SCREWED,
BLU'D AND
TATTOOED

SCREWED, BLU'D AND TATTOOED

And Other Stories

Reef Perkins

ABSOLUTELY AMAZING eBOOKS

ABSOLUTELY AMAZING eBOOKS

Published by Whiz Bang LLC, 926 Truman Avenue, Key West, Florida 33040, USA

For information contact:
Publisher@AbsolutelyAmazingEbooks.com
ISBN-13: 978-0615925103
ISBN-10: 0615925103

For Roberta

"I just might be the lunatic you're looking for."

Billy Joel

There is little useful information in this book. I made up some words. Most of the facts are wrong. Some of the timing is off and all emotions are temporary. No fictional turtles, dogs, stink-bugs, birds or worms where harmed during the writing. Except for the fly, the fly was real and for that I am sorry.

The story is from a place between the sheets, the sheets of bullshit and belief. A half-awake daydream trapped under an upturned wine glass.

Read, and be unfettered by the high velocity of reason, the buzz killing stench of common sense or the sticky residue of reality.

Hop onboard the Ford, for words are, in the end, only ink.

Written on location,
REEF PERKINS
KEY WEST 2013

ACKNOWLEDGMENTS

I would like to thank the many, the brave, who helped me catch a wave on the first book. This time, some of the "many" saw me coming and went on vacation. And a belated thanks to an unknown stenographer in western Canada who endured the "early work."

Still, folks like Shirrel Rhoades, Robin Robinson, Leah Benner, Kathy Russ, Joan Langley, Quincy Perkins, Michael Haskins, and Charlie and the Smokin' Tuna Tribe stayed in the game and kept me away from literary fly strips. They helped pull me through on this one.

Thanks to all and especially Roberta who, with fine humor, gentle understanding, great hope and well concealed disbelief, listened to this story come to life.

We all should have such friends.

CONTENTS

SCREWED, BLU'D AND TATTOOED

Screwed, Blu'd and Tattooed
"Two roads forked in a wood.
I don't care what roads do in private.
I turned and headed back. It was cold.
And that has made no difference at all."

(Blu Yunger, 8th grade)

FOREFINGER

by
Blu Yunger

Some souls are destined to wander without a clue. I am one, one of many. My name is Blu Yunger. I lost my left ear in an apple-bobbing contest. I am the raffle prize no one wants, the short straw, the single sock, the inappropriate noise. Skinny as a stick, with my own red hair, some teeth and several unproven ideas, I am all that I can be and will be myself since, as they say, all the others are taken.

To be made aware of one's mistakes is difficult at best but having an untrained fool write about them is an undertaking I would prefer not to endure, but must. But must, but must, but must ... I don't know why I do that but, be assured I will protect my dignity, which may be called into question, with great vigor and ... but must, but must ... but look, I didn't know I was going to be in this book, neither did you, so let's cut the crap. It's me, Blu, and I want you with me on this one.

THE EARLY BIRD CASINO

MIAMI, FLORIDA

B lu Yunger rocketed through the parking lot in a 1955 Ford Fairlane. The fast moving car swept the crushed coral road. An unwary ibis was sucked up by the vehicle's slipstream and driven ass-first into a stout Frangipani tree with a squawk. The singular note united with fine coral particles and fluttering bingo debris to cloak the ungainly fowl. The license plate read: JUS-1-MO.

Nearby, under a streetlight, an elderly woman paused on a carpet of crushed crustaceans that constituted the parking lot of the Early Bird Casino. She mumbled gently in the soft ocean air and rummaged for her keys. A familiar looking Ford whizzed by. "Oh, for Land's Sake, that looks like my car!"

She too was dusted with sparkling particles and, for an instant, resembled a large Tinker Bell in the bright incandescent light. The old lady sneezed and looked for a tissue. She peered into her purse, dug deeper and inadvertently discharged her mace.

≈≈≈

Forgive and forget, there's a reason why they put them

words in that order, Blu thought ... if you forgive, it's easier to forget, otherwise you might forget to forgive. He remembered hearing those words, or some like them, in a church once and truly hoped to be forgiven for stealing the car. Forgiven but not forgotten. Sure, he felt sorry for the old lady, but Blu was not one to live a life of regret. Early on he promised himself that his time on earth would not be a dry-hump. His hungry mind turned, like a windsock in the rain.

Blu stepped on the gas and limbo'd the commandeered car under the rising gate arm. He swallowed with excitement, adjusted the rearview mirror and floored the Ford. Somehow he missed a squad of Snorkel-Beaked Grebes feeding on flattened bugs near the exit. Blu *carpe'd* the moment, hung a left and caught a glimpse of his bobbing Adam's apple in the rear view mirror. "Bingo, Bango!" His words were stolen by the wind and the scent of southern oceans embraced his dilated nostrils. Startled nose hairs whistled a salty tune and Blu let his imagination go, knowing full well it might not return. He talked to himself even when he wasn't listening.

Blu turned left, but knew from experience that he was headed right. Maybe my new life just started, Blu thought and goosed the Ford. "OK, here goes," Blu said it softly, testing the humor of tropic air, "Mat me and frame me, it's time for the wall, the blind man winked at the man with three balls." He liked to make up sayings but usually said them quietly to himself, not sure of how good they were and yet, he knew his time would come. He was waiting for something. He kept waiting.

The night air was warm, the Ford was fast and ill-fated

bugs peppered the windshield like funky buckshot. Miami felt good. So did Blu.

The stolen Ford ran real smooth and anyway, it was all downhill from Miami to Key West.

Previous Deeds

Blu Yunger grew up in Hinckley, Ohio, seasonal home of the Hinckley buzzard. The Hinckley is a cosmopolitan scavenger that every year, for reasons unknown, migrates to Key West to shit upon the tropical paradise at will. Some Hincklanders called the turkey buzzards, "turd smugglers."

Blu was born long and skinny with a hefty Adam's apple, curly red hair and a third testicle. According to his mom, the attending midwife said the triple was an "O-Man!" The auxiliary orb eventually caused Blu to walk like an old cowboy.

After three years in third grade and problems with punctuation, primarily hyphens, Blu's hope, (he only had one,) began to fade but his curiosity was as insatiable and indiscriminant as fire. He always remembered what Mr. Bork, his ninth grade English teacher told him. "Young Yunger," Bork leaned over, "Stop and look at the greatest works of art in the world then, look at your own work. Which do you like best? I rest my case." Bork patted Blu on the back and walked away with a knowing smile.

Unfortunately, but predictably, Blu liked neither his own work nor that of anyone else, including the too familiar Bork. Fortunately, this intellectual set back failed to disturb Blu and his education still proved to be worthwhile because, in the tenth grade, he discovered that if you said a word over and over it eventually made no sense at all. This knowledge was a constant, his first knowledge, and Blu became a slave to this God-given understanding. The words doily, dwarf and hoof were his favorites at the time and there were others, of course, but in the end he settled on hoof as his default word. He couldn't remember the others anymore and used to think his lack of short-term memory was funny, until he forgot why.

At age twenty-one, Blu graduated from high school with a wrinkled diploma, a bad case of zits and a serious disregard for conventional wisdom. This led to short-term work in a number of jobs including bocce ball pit man, slot machine hopper, hog slopper, mung bean picker and later as a vector control officer. Blu looked "vector" up in the dictionary, after he got the job. The first definition he found read, "A genetics agent such as a plasmid or bacteriophage that is used in genetic modification to transfer a segment of foreign DNA into a bacterium or other cell."

Blu felt challenged and a little pissed. All that work for nine bucks an hour? He thought he was supposed to point at things or kill bugs, but he was an Officer and got to wear a uniform, so he stayed a year. The only thing Blu could do with certainty was cast a shadow and even then things didn't always go his way in this florescent light world.

At age twenty-seven Blu pulled three weeks jail time in the Hinckley Hard House for Unruly Humans. He got nabbed stealing a burglar alarm kit from the *On Sale* rack at Radio Shack.

He never forgot *that* night in the shower.

A bunch of soapy, wet guys surrounded him and looked at his third orb. One persistent observer of misery, Jimmy Ray Bobray, produced a waterproof camera and took several pictures. He later mailed one of the photos to Blu's ex-girl friend, a shot from Blu's waist down to his knees.

Her unexpected reply arrived at the Hard House in a scented envelope. "I don't like the way they cut your hair, Blu," she wrote, "it makes your nose look too long." Everyone laughed and got to sniff the envelope. To help the hard time pass, Blu played Domino. He only had one. It was sad to watch.

On Blu's last night in jail, a con, or possibly a perp, named Hunk Gunderson offered to give Blu a time-honored jailhouse tattoo. Hunk had his own tat. Across Hunk's broad back Blu had seen a black-inked snake and the words "...tread on me." Before Blu could comment Hunk explained, "The Don't word wore off from sleeping on my left side too much. "

Blu stuck his arm through the bars and into the adjacent cell. After two hours he pulled it back and stared at his new tat. It was done with a sharpened shoelace tip and dense purple dye from grape Jell-O that the Hunkster cooked down. The tat read, Born To Loose. Blu mentioned the spelling error to Hunk.

"Don't worry about it man, I was into O's. Dat extra O is free on me."

Blu passed Hunk a half-full roll of toilet paper as a thank you.

He was released and after twenty-one days of rehab in the Witless Protection Program, Blu rejoined the general population. He reviewed his options and decided to follow the turkey buzzards south for the winter.

Ugly enough to blend in most places, Blu migrated to Florida where he ended up hanging with Q-tips and blue hairs on Miami Beach. The older women loved his red hair and tried to snatch it out. He learned to keep it short.

Blu looked for God but found Bingo instead. *BINGO,* just the word made his shorts tight. He often pronounced the word backwards, *OGNIB, t*o avoid making a scene.

Blu became a player and was eventually invited to attend the exclusive *All You Can Eat-Early Worm Special,* gaming sessions held in the fashionable Wrinkle City Room at the Early Bird Casino.

To make a little pocket change at the Wrinkle, Blu charged some of the more mature ladies five bucks for the opportunity to look at, photograph and even mail close-up pictures of his third orb to interested parties. He usually started by unfolding his special one-man photo-tent and setting up the "U-Pick-Em" sign that his clients loved. "It's a gift," Blu told his customers in advance, nipping unseemly questions in the bud.

Taking cash, jump-starting a few pacemakers, selling envelopes, even stamps and signing Polaroid photos, Blu had his first taste of fame.

Finally, one night, his night, Blu won a four-hundred dollar jackpot in the Wrinkle City Room. Four-hundred dollars! In high spirits Blu Yunger borrowed the Ford.

Present

L ater that night, after counting his four-hundred dollar jackpot for the eighth time, Blu stole a license plate off an old Yugo parked ass-in near a Guzzle gas station in South Miami. He tweaked the stolen plate onto the Ford then reclined, thumbed through his wad for the ninth time, and watched a watchable girl in cut-off blue jeans punch a handful of quarters into a nearby air pump. The girl had skinny, swizzle-stick legs stuck in a pair of oversized, fire engine red sling back pumps, nicely showcased by a pair of pale white anklets. The right anklet read *Today*, the left read *Tomorrow*. Her long dark hair was pulled back in a ponytail and tied with a plastic shopping bag. Blu read the words "**PUBIX Superma**" on the wrinkled sack.

The young woman thumbed in a few more coins then cut the end off the air hose with a small switchblade. The polished blade flashed a spectrum of light into Blu's hungry eyes when she snapped it closed. Her puckered lips were stop-sign red. Blu involuntarily pushed on the brakes.

Air-girl adjusted her well-articulated butt, pigeon-toed her sling backs for balance and stuffed the flailing hose down the front of her stained, "Just Vote No" crenulated tank top.

It was good. There was crenulation aplenty.

The she-god stood quietly, feet apart and let the solid air bluster between her bubbering breasts, down through her waistband and finally out to an unwanted freedom at the bottom of her cut-off jeans. Time inhaled the beauty, so did Blu. The funneled breeze cleared the area below. Discarded condom wrappers, lottery tickets, dreams and pop-tops ran for cover.

The girl threw her head back and drank from a brown paper bag. It was wet on the bottom. Blu liked her style.

She'd seen him watching. She'd seen the brake lights flash. When the air ran out she came straight over to his car. Blu tucked the wad of cash under his ass and looked away as she approached. He pretended to search for a breath mint. The girl put her elbows on the hood, pulled the driver's-side windshield wiper and let it snap back, almost shattering the glass. Blu calmly looked up.

"You got any quarters?" she asked.

"Nope. Ah, what's your name?"

"Fuck Ya! I need air!" she said and moved away.

Blu had difficulty rolling his window down and opened his door instead. "Fakyah Aineedair?" he repeated sweetly.

"Yeah?" She turned like a runway model and laughed. Blu never had an Arab before. The girl's name sounded exotic, like a place with sand and camels and bullets. Blu smiled bigger and hoped the girl spoke English. He reached across to open the passenger door. "Hop in Fakyah, I'm Blu, and I know where there's plenty of free air or, we can make our own!"

Fakyah hopped in the Ford and checked her lipstick in the rear view mirror. Blu watched her fluid moves. "Don't go no-where's," he said and ran into the convenience store to buy a few items. Fakyah paused, looked down, then yelled out Blu's partly open window, "Hey slick, is this your wad?"

Blu's mother always said, "If you figure out you're fucked-up when you're young, it won't come as such surprise when you get old." Blu didn't know why he remembered her words at this moment, or any other moment, for that matter.

≈ ≈ ≈

Four days after the vehicle theft, a report was filed in the *Miami Cherub Newspaper*, a local rag that catered to dead voters and came out twice a year. The report said in part... "A *Mr. B. Yunger, age unknown, is wanted for questioning in connection with a Ford theft at a local bingo parlor. Anyone knowing the whereabouts of Mr. Yunger is asked to contact the local police or shoot him on sight.*"

No charges were filed at that time.

Later, a pigmented barber in Liberty City was interviewed by the same *Cherub,* "small and meaningless crimes," reporter. The barber, Jimmy Ray Bobray, knew Blu from his own prison days and had saved a copy of a photo, the one from the shower. He showed it to the reporter and his production crew.

"CUT!" the red-faced reporter yelled at his cameraman, "That nasty picture don't help us much, Sir!" he snapped at Jimmy Ray Bobray.

Unfortunately, Bobray was un-snappable. He pointed at the picture again and held it up to the camera, "It was, jezz ... he cain't make his own-self to stop, that kind of a thang ... He was a story, that one. Whooee! Crazy as bat shit. Course, he got three balls and it don't matter now anyway, but what he toad me sure sounded crazy e-nuff to be true...It was like he knew into the time, the time ahead, man."

"CUT!"

Ingrown Heirs

A Compact History

B lu's Yunger's far-flung uncle, Ferling Bagwidth, once described as a "hermit crab without the personality," owned a home and clock repair shop half way down Dung Beetle Lane in Old Town, Key West. Ferling was a Conch. A Conch (pronounced Konk) is someone born, without a say in the matter, on the island of Key West.

One hundred years ago Ferling's great uncle, Wiley Bagwidth, a Bahamian and Master Shipwright, along with his partner, Moon Bender, had dismantled a ramshackle bordello on Old Guano Cay, in the southern Bahamas. They shipped the pieces to the Isle of Bones on a turtle schooner, along with one hundred roosters, and reassembled it on Dung Beetle lane. Unfortunately, some wooden pieces were used to make a cooking fire to fry chicken during the voyage. It was a long trip and a hungry crew. Only two of the one-hundred roosters made it ashore and, in a tragic oversight, Moon Bender forgot to bring any hens. The roosters made do.

Over the years Bagwidth learned that Key West was originally discovered by a gay Spaniard who, after an unusually long crossing, affectionately and accordingly named the barren rock *Cayo Hueser*, the Isle of Boners, as a tribute to his crew. However, upon his return to Spain, the name caused great public uproar and unwarranted pain to the captain and crew and, although many clergy suddenly volunteered for sea duty, the name was quickly modified by scribes to read, *Cayo Hueso*, the Isle of Bones.

Present

O n this early spring morning Ferling Bagwidth sat in his office on the second floor of the rundown Conch structure. Ferling Bagwidth was short and rotund and, although gravity cursed him, had no fear of it or respect for it. Gravity met another non-believer and smiled gently.

Bagwidth looked around the old Conch house, his home for many years. On quiet mornings he sometimes wished the crew had not cooked so much chicken during the voyage. He missed having a back wall, not to mention doors. On this particular morning however, Ferling Bagwidth finished his *café con leche* and walked boldly out and onto his front porch.

Ferling's fingers, gnarled from years of dicking around, curled tightly on the grips of his self-activating, percussion powered Pogo stick. The Self-Activating Pogo Stick (SAPS) had been Bagwidth's dream project for many years. He tried to market it to the US Army during various skirmishes. No dice, something about "sand, rice paddies, snow..." stopped the deal, as he recalled. But now, war was much more civilized and fought on paved city streets with gas guzzling weapons and nice outfits. He imagined a platoon of warriors charging an enemy camp on Pogo sticks. Employing this mental picture he remained dedicated to his dream, his pathway to riches.

Bagwidth's prototype Pogo stick, named Looner-Too,

was a stroke of genius. Powered by fifty .22 caliber blank rifle shells, a stainless steel disc near the bottom rotated as the rider went up and a new shell came into place. The firing pin was made out of an old clock pendulum bob. Down and Bang! The explosion theoretically sent the stick and pilot some twenty feet in the air and, theoretically, twenty to fifty feet forward. Of course, the fatter the pilot the greater the compression and Bagwidth was a fat Ace who longed to escape the surly blonds of earth. A successful flight depended on the skill and daring of the pilot.

Ferling gripped the shaft firmly and circled his thumb and forefinger in the spirit of Yoga-Zen-Buddha books. He took a series of deep breaths through his hair-laden nostrils. Bagwidth liked the whistling sound they made, like small jet engines spooling up. He was almost ready for takeoff when he ingested a fruit fly. Bagwidth coughed violently and shot his false teeth into the herb planter near the railing. The fly was vented to safety, but the airborne denture took out two basils and an immature mint plant on the way down. Still, nothing would stop Bagwidth this day.

Ferling didn't need to chew anything anyway. "All I want to eat is AIR!" he gummed. He was feeling good. It was early morning, just past dawn. "It's a good day, a good day to die!" He flapped his gums and yelled at the neighbors, who quickly gathered on their porches to observe Mr. Ferling Bagwidth's biannual attempt to "Get'er done!" To perfect his Pogo stick or, die trying. Looner-Too was stenciled in black on the non-magnetic shaft.

"Think I'll give her a go!" he always screamed, and screamed again as he prepared to vault down Dung Beetle Lane and into someone's life.

Over the years, Bagwidth had been removed from garbage cans, kitty litter trays, old tires, swimming pools and the lower fronds of a Dwarf Malayan palm tree where he had remained for eight hours, ass out, being consistently mistaken for a clump of coconuts and needlessly prodded by curious tourists.

After eighteen years of "insincere attempts," as the cops referred to the incidents, the police stopped showing up and some people cut the top off their pickets wanting to avoid liability. But the Conch kids kept selling tickets to unwary tourists.

Bagwidth was getting old and feared today's test run. His knees were bad from Bocce ball. But, yet, and still, there was always the chance that today was the day. The neighbors were out in force and ready for his run, mimosas and legal sized scorecards in hand. Bagwidth had never scored more than 3 out of 10 during previous attempts.

He strapped his helmet and groin cup on. (The neighbors thought it funny when he got them mixed up.) Bagwidth looked at the eager faces awaiting takeoff and he began the launch sequence. He locked his knees and thought back to his own family and how he would miss them if he didn't make it. Would they miss him? Probably not, they're all dead, Bagwidth recalled and watched the time around him expand, every second a minute, every minute an hour.

He'd have to watch out for slow moving neutrinos.

"Think I'll give her a go!" And give her a go he did.

Bagwidth History

Years ago, Ferling's father, Big Roid Bagwidth, sent him a handwritten letter. It was the only communication Ferling received from his father since Big Roid went out for diapers fifty some years ago and, although Ferling didn't know it at the time, he received the letter just days after Big Roid died.

Big Roid's simple two-page note to his son began, "I guano die now." The first and only letter from his father also informed Ferling that the Bagwidth Clan had been highly respected guano farmers in the Bahamas since the early eighteen hundreds, but the demand for guano, used in making explosives, had fallen off and dried up after the First World War and the family's fortune turned to shit.

A month after Big Roid's unscheduled departure, Ferling's mom, Moonbeam Iota, called from a phone booth in Minot, North Dakota. She sounded drunk and kept calling him "Furring." She told Ferling that his dad, Big Roid, had run a hose from the family car's exhaust pipe through the driver's side window and into the front seat. Unfortunately, she went on to say, the hose came off the exhaust pipe and Big Roid froze to death trying to commit suicide. "The fuel gauge was on empty and the heater was off when I found his ass, so going to the store for cigarettes just had to wait." She paused, "Your dad was the only man I ever knew that could fuck up a fuck-up."

She further reported that Big Roid had been cremated in a steel, fifty-five gallon drum, fish-smoker behind Dirty Daryl's BBQ Pit in Minot. It was cold in Minot. The cremation took three days. "They was runnin' low on dry wood toward the end and hadta' pour some gas on his ass," his mom paused and Blu heard another coin drop into the pay phone slot. "After Roid was scooped out, the cooker smelled so bad the guys tried to bury it but the damn ground was froze. So they gave it to me. I had to stare at the fucking thing all winter."

When he was young, Ferling's mom, Moonbeam, was frequently confronted by disturbed neighbors who were tired of weird goings-on in the area. They often asked, "What was that kid thinking?" His mom got up, brushed the ashes off her half-buttoned kimono, pulled the TV guide out of her bra, set her uppers in drive and said, "Yep, you got that one right, *dickweed*...ain't no one thinks like my Ferling do." His mom loved him and called him "my little earthling."

Moonbeam never fully recovered from Big Roid's death, or life for that matter, and lived in a confused state until her own demise, the result of a rabid beaver attack, a few years later.

Two years after they planted Moonbeam Iota, Big Roid's ashes were delivered to Dung Beetle Lane and have since resided in a Mason jar labeled *dAD*. His remains served as a paperweight for unpaid bills.

Big Roid's finally good for something, was a mean-spirited thought Ferling occasionally embraced. He missed Moonbeam but it was time to launch and Ferling's familial daydream fizzled to a stop.

On the Porch

Back on the porch, Ferling Bagwidth checked his cup, focused his eyes and mounted the Looner-Too. With a sense of history and a deep breath, Bagwidth made the first small hop for mankind. BAM! The blank fired perfectly, launching him twenty feet up, and down, Dung Beetle Lane. Bagwidth leaned into the wind; he felt good, real good and prepared for a one point landing ... *BANG!* He nailed it; the second blank went off right on time. "FLAPS UP-GEAR UP!" Bagwidth screamed and was on his way.

"It's a goddamned miracle! I'm rich, I'm rich!" he hollered and checked the scorecards as he cleared the end of Dung Beetle lane. Was that a 10 he saw? Only three blanks fired and already he was headed for the open road.

Bagwidth was well on his way to Stark Island when he caught a bad rise on Flagler Avenue and landed on the gleaming hood of a perfectly restored, candy-apple red, 1965 Chevy Camaro convertible.

"Sorry, amigo!" Ferling yelled at a rotund Latin who slammed on his brakes and got smacked in the back of the head with a set golf clubs.

The next shell detonated.

Bagwidth kept going. He had to. "How can I stop now?" he yelled. It was a question that should have been posed much earlier in the research and development process. Eventually, Bagwidth ended up in the mangroves near the golf course, where he landed the Looner-Too. Bagwidth brought the stick in like a pilot on a night aircraft carrier landing. "Fly the Balls!" he screeched and touched down in three-feet of mangrove mud. He still had one blank left.

He'd made it, it worked, and he would be rich. "I fuckin' did it!" His voice echoed through the mangroves behind the county jail.

Bagwidth was on a roll. He recovered the Looner and made his way eastward toward the looming majesty of the old city dump. Known locally as Mount Trashmore, the fertile mound was an unsightly organic hump with a smelly shadow and a family attraction for carrion.

Ferling needed to absorb his success and made the undemanding climb up the south face. "Land of the Clods," Ferling called it. It was the place he liked to go, to get away from it all. One of the few spots the Conch Train didn't go, but eventually would. He climbed, crab-like, to the craggy windswept peak, squatted down and faced into the prevailing southeasterly trade winds. The swerving seagulls swooped close, then pulled away screeching, leaving delicate downy drafts of weathered white butt feathers, like tropical snowflakes, spinnerolling around him.

The flapping turkey vultures circled majestically aloft, riding the updrafts. Guano from heaven rained about him. It never failed; it was always peaceful and nostalgic. He was home. "Stanks, don't it?" he intoned to the spirits. He thought he heard someone banging on a pipe in the distance.

Back in the Ford

The Ford Fairlane ran cool at ninety-five miles an hour on the Florida Turnpike and there *was* plenty of air. The damp, dirt-scented breeze sucked fast through the Ford and bitch-slapped a green Pine Tree deodorizer hanging from Fakyah's middle finger. Blu bought the stinky tree and a six-pack of Schlitz at the Guzzle gas station. He was trying to soften her up and more importantly, get rid of the old lady lavender scent in the car. The smell reminded him of his grandmother. He loved Granny but hated the smell of lavender. It made him sad.

He glanced at Fakyah. Every time Blu saw a woman, he liked to think about what love is, or could be. He already knew it was easier to love than to be loved. You can love somebody then just up and quit but, if someone loves you, and you let them, it's not as easy to bail. Blu leaned toward Fakyah and inhaled deeply. She smelled of compressed air, pine tree, gasoline and beer. Blu loved her; he went first and it was easy.

Fakyah held her slim right hand out the window and watched the stinky Christmas tree spin until it twisted tight and turned her middle fingertip pink. She pulled her hand back and showed Blu her middle finger. Blu noticed some indiscernible markings on her knuckles. She took a good whiff of the 'Pine,' then let it spin back the other way. It was her emotional gyrocompass.

Blu whistled a salty tune to avoid being hypnotized. He reached down the front of his shorts, paused briefly and retrieved his secret herb stash, duct taped to his inner left thigh. "Ouch!" Blu croaked. Fakyah pinched her lips, snorted and looked away. Blu fingered the roll of twenties on the way out of his shorts then fumbled for, fondled, and finally fired off a well-rolled spliff.

"Last of the cars with good side vents," Fakyah said through the pungent haze. Her backlit green eyes tracked Blu like a helicopter spotlight in a cop show.

Blu took another toke, "Cars, danged if you ain't right, Fakyah, this one here's a 1955 Ferd Furlane." He exhaled a small cumulus. "I love cars."

"No shit ... Smoke?"

"Fuck yes ... Toke?"

It was quiet. It was good, but the traffic was making Blu nervous. He exited onto US Highway 1.

Fakyah leaned forward, blew a nimbus and stared at a smattered bug on the windshield. "It wasn't right to go off and leave him like that. I'm sure gonna get it if I go back." She said the words flatly, through a mouthful of her own hair. "Silly-ass-asshole was limpin' around the kitchen holding his damn foot and crying like a baby...'Hep me! Hep me!' ... I guess it hurt. I guess it did, and I guess I shouldn't a-been listening to my favorite song right then neither ... that's what did it, the song!"

"What song is that?" Blu asked.

"It's by Lisa Carver. You know that one that goes ...

≈≈≈

'Lookin' back now, I probably shoulda let him run ...
Paybacks are hell where I come from ...

Any fool should know you don't look a woman in the
  eye, and smile ...
When she knows what you've done...
And she's holding ... whiskey and a gun.'

It's a good song. But, godammit, I shoulda pulled the trigger again, I sure as shit shoulda! What's one more fucking bullet, Blu?"

What diddydo, what diddydo? Blu wondered and hoped not to make the same mistake.

Blu pushed hard on the Ford's spring loaded gas pedal. He was barefoot, one big toe on the brake and one big toe on the gas, to reduce confusion. They headed south. You have to be tough to drive these old ones...why didn't someone leave the keys in a danged Mercedes? He pondered while his toes numbed and countless asphalt cracks barked like mean little dogs at the intruding tires.

The faster you go, the quicker you become history Blu thought and pushed on the gas. He wanted to be history. Everybody knew history and Blu wanted to be known. Blu wanted to be a hero. Feeling inspired he remembered an old saying; "The more coffee you drink the quicker you do stupid things." It had a ring to it. He tried to think. Suddenly he wanted coffee. He was penting up.

After a few minutes, Fakyah pulled her hand in and Blu got a good look at her fingers. The markings he'd noticed earlier were in fact a crude tattoo across the back of her knuckles. The letters KCUF were printed in dark blue ink. Fakyah noticed Blu's inquisitive glance. "I did it myself using a mirror," she said proudly and held her hand up to the rearview mirror. Blu could read it now. Fakyah continued, "First, the sumbitch runs outta gas going uphill. I mean... that's dumb, Blu, just plain dumb...gas goes to the back of the tank ... going uphill, don't it. Life seems realer going uphill...don't it, Blu, don't it ... Blu?" Fakyah exhaled a perfect smoky "O" toward Blu's heart. He reached for it and it disappeared. That's life in a nutshell, Blu said to himself. Well, at least there are no hills from here to Key West. Did she say doughnut? The thought made him hungry. He nodded his head in agreement. It was a safe answer, but Fakyah didn't see him.

Blu was tired and wiggled his ear, engaged his brain and tried to stay awake. He liked the pain of thinking. No pain, no brain. Maybe *it's* just started. Blu knew only too well that the *It* of life, the *It* that changes everything, the *It* you don't see coming, could appear at any given moment.

Suddenly Blu's eyes parted. He was uneasy. Could this be *It*? Involuntarily, Blu responded to himself but not quite sure of the correct move, stalled for time by breathing in through his nose and out through his butt, an ancient calming technique gleaned from a discarded yoga manual.

Problem solved. Yoga works. But it wasn't the *It*.

With a furtive glance at Blu, Fakyah stuck her face out the window.

"Yoga," Blu said by way of an explanation.

"Yoga, huh?... Stanks, don't, ... ackk ...!" Fakyah ingested a stink-bug at fifty-miles an hour and choked. "Ackk ... ackk." Blu careened off the highway, hoping to perform a customized Heimlich maneuver. Fakyah hasped, like a cat with a hairball. She finally power-gagged and ejected the unwanted insect onto Blu's shirt.

The missed opportunity disturbed Blu's drain of thought as he pulled back on to US 1.

Even though the Pine Thang was helpful at the moment, Blu wished he had bought Fakyah some lip-gloss instead. He wanted to impress her with his couth. His mind wandered like a slug on a hot sidewalk. Maybe he'd give "The Pine Stinker" to his Uncle Bagwidth when he got to Key West. "Always solve the hardest problem first," his mom used to say. No one knew why she said it.

But then, in that moment, all was right with the world. Blu was falling in love. Together Blu and Fakyah rocketed through the fecund fields of Homestead. Blu scratched himself and listened to a tiny violin near his ear. The music was beautiful, jus' like love. The music, however, stopped abruptly when Blu slapped at the side of his head. The melodic skeeter had nowhere to run.

Blu dug the crumpled mosquito carcass out of his missing ear hole and yelled blindly out the window, "Buncha needle, hyphen, dick, hyphen, bug fuckers, I cain't take it no more! Man, if it wasn't for the wind... ("He always had to blame someone else for his shortcomings," his mother used to say) ...man if it wasn't for the wind, I'd do something really big." Blu couldn't stop thinking and his brain hurt. That bug pissed him off. No respect. "I don't want to be knowed as a goll-hyphen-darned red neck," he wailed and turned to face Fakyah.

"It's OK, Blu, I git it," she said softly, impressed with Blu's bold and unexpected use of hyphens. "Where's your left ear, man?"

"Lost it in an apple bobbing contest at the 4H," he said

31

with some embarrassment.

Fakyah turned her head and served a one-hundred-mile-per-hour smile, "You ain't no red neck, Blu, you're a scarlet nape," but the smile was a net ball. Horns blared, tires screamed and the water smelled warmer because she liked him. "I jez don't want to live with a bunch of frog fuckers!" Blu hoped his outburst helped Fakyah understand him. He was...

≈≈≈

"We going ...we going do some crazy shit now, Fakyah, and if'n we don't ... why ... you'd tell me ... Right?" he asked, knowing she wanted to and would.

Fakyah flashed a stop sign smile and a billion, fun-loving neurons rushed the gates of conventional thinking. It was Spring Break for brains.

≈≈≈

Blu got excited and decided to practice his frog-kick. His antics made the car swerve wildly. "I usually sit around trying to pick up old whores with a promise rig," he winked, careening across the double yellow line, "amazing what some folk do believe. You need bait? Rig ? ... cuz baby we going fishing."

Fakyah smiled more, "Gotta git yourself right-sized, Blu-man... so things don't get out of hand...you'll want a leader, baby, so nothing *bites your bait off*, ... an' Blu Man... open that window some more for me...more, more...baby, more. You promise?" She pointed at him with her middle finger, the Pine Tree still spun slowly on its own. She knows he likes her.

"Dang it, now she's got me." Blu muttered and struggled to roll the window down. It struck half way.

"That promise rig thang always bites me back."

"Stanks, don't it," Fakyah said to her middle finger.

Blu changed the subject and showed Fakyah one of a hundred dead stink- bugs smashed on the front window. He pointed at the greasy smatter and laughed, "Takes guts to do that." It was an old joke and getting older by the day.

"Stanks," Fakyah responded, trying to show some emotion and keep the conversation going. Blu looked at her. It's more than me now, he thought, it's about me and Fakyah...Bingo! He had an idea, but lost it.

≈≈≈

On down the road it took Blu some time to refocus after they stopped for fries at a Burger Thing near Rude Quail Road. There was a scuffle on the way out when Blu tried to keep Fakyah from stealing all the ketchup packets. Still, she got away with a pretty good tank top full. He could read the word Heinz on a single-serve packet over her involuntarily trapped, oxygen-starved nipple that fought for survival beneath the crenulating cotton.

"We gonna need these later," she winked and caught Blu gawking at her packets. His face turned Heinz red. He goosed the Furlane and sprayed pea rock on a Budweiser truck pulling up behind them.

Later, after re-organizing and rationing the remaining packets, a rotund waitress at the Burger Thing reported to the manager. "Lordy, Lordy... if that fool boy hadn't holt on to that girl, she'da cleaned us out! Seems it's gonna take more than the truth to change that boy's mind. Lordy Lordy...Why chil'...once that girl took it in her head ... WhoooWee! Just like a fart in a bathtub, there weren't no stopping her. Watch Out!"

≈≈≈

Blu Yunger looked down the ever-narrowing highway and howled at the windshield, "Hey dick-weed! ... dim yer' freakin' lights, there's so many thing's out there and they're all coming this way, it's either shit or go blind," all without taking a breath. "Maybe *It* just started," he wanted to shout, but gasped for air instead.

By now Fakyah got the picture and Blu knew it. She was curled up like a mole beside him. She stretched and put her head in his lap. Blu lost focus but his eyesight returned quickly when the engine coughed like an old whore in a biker bar. Blu turned right and coasted to a stop at Bad Mel's gas station. EMPTY.

"We're in Leisure City, there's rain and a stoplight and a dirty word on a wall," he noted as way of a travelogue. Fakyah seemed uninterested.

Blu Yunger needed food, he was sick of ketchup, he wanted to chew. He got gas instead.

They pulled away from the pump and Fakyah put her head back in Blu's lap. She looked up at him. Her puffy chinchilla eyes were mostly closed. The tip of her wet pink tongue stuck out between her stop-sign lips. Without opening her mouth she mumbled, "Ithinkikindalikeyoublu." At least that's what it sounded like to Blu. Fakyah was drooling, but still, it was enough for now. Blu pushed her tongue back in with his index finger and left it there for a moment.

≈≈≈

It was early morning when Blu and Fakyah coasted to a stop in the parking lot of The Last Gasp Bar, south of Homestead. They finished the Schlitz and took a nap.

When they awoke they were still a hundred miles from Key West and out of beer. Blu looked at Fakyah and Fakyah looked at Blu's reflection looking at her in the rear view mirror.

"Where'd you get this Ferd?" she asked the mirror.

"It was just waiting for me, baby, the *Keys* were in it," he said with a satisfied smirk thinking, "dang...she sure do speak good American for an A-rab."

"I like how you lie, Blu. Oh an' you do! Let's go an' see what's comin' next, an' let's catch us some too!" Blu went into the Last Gasp to get beer and a few pickled eggs. Fakyah went into the bushes to pee. The mosquitoes were bad.

Back in the Ferd, Fakyah scratched her privates while Blu tapped the fuel gauge with his bony knuckle. He stepped on the gas. The G force sent both Fakyah and the red gas needle bouncing backwards, the fuel gauge recovered to settle at half full. They were underway, the entrance to the Keys in sight. It would be a good day. Blu was an optimist like his flatulent mom. "My gas is half full," she always used to say. They popped a pop-top. The Keys looked to be downhill when he started, but now Blu stared at a barrier made out of stacked coconuts hastily installed by the US Border Patrol.

It was an international border on US Highway 1 and meant to keep aliens and smugglers in, or out of, the Florida Keys. The Feds weren't sure which.

The tropic sun boned down and warmed the oil-slicked asphalt as Blu pulled up to the checkpoint. Fakyah was pretending to be asleep. He hoped his hot license plate was still fresh. A Border Patrol agent waved him to a stop in front of the newly constructed barrier. Blu quaffed his brew and hid the can under his seat.

The stubby agent approached and stared in through the window. Blu's thin hairs stood up. The fat ones remained seated. The Agent looked across the front seat at the sleeping girl and then pointed through the window toward Blu's crotch. Blu was stunned; he wasn't even in Key West yet! The agent tapped the window like a woodpecker and pointed down again, Blu followed the trajectory of the agent's sun burnt, but well manicured finger. "Crank it, son!" said the agent. These old cars are tough, Blu thought. He struggled with the handle and again the window creaked slowly downward.

"Where ya'll headed?" the agent asked through the crack at the top and looked over at Fakyah.

"We're going to Key West to check out my old uncle Bagwidth," Blu said through the gap.

"Bagwidth... aye...don't know the name. Anyways, do you know why I stopped you?"

"Bad breath?" Blu countered.

"No, son, see this here's a road block, an..." he pointed at the pyramid-shaped stacks of coconuts in front of the Fairlane, "an so I'll needta see some ID." The agent paused, narrowed his eyes and leaned forward, "You got an ID, son?"

An idea? What idea? Blu thought. Maybe the agent hoped he was going to make a run for it and wanted to shoot him in the back, like in the movies.

"Well, ah, I ain't got no ideas, officer sir," Blu said carefully. The agent shook his head, "What's the girl's name?" he said, noticing a strong pine scent coming from the car.

"Fakyah," Blu replied.

The agent's face reddened, he reached for his gun and ordered Blu to get out of the car. At that moment, a four-foot-long, forty-pound iguana thrashed out of the bush, ran across the warming asphalt, spun around and came to a stop between the agent's legs. The iguana loved warm asphalt on its cold reptilian ass and the agent's shadow shielded its warted eyes from the boning sun. The reptile looked up at toward at the agent's uniformed crotch. It slithered closer and flicked its quick tongue in and out, missing the agent's equipment by an inch. The agent froze. His pocket python would be no match for the iguana. It was early. His partner was asleep in the patrol car down the road with the AC and AM radio on.

The agent looked at Blu. He knew if Blu opened the door, as ordered by a lawful person, it would hit the iguana in the ass and spook the hefty reptile. So did Blu. "Drive awaay slooowly," said the agent, whose voice had changed noticeably, "reeeeal slow."

"Yes sir, officer, sir!" Blu grinned and gunned the Furlane. He sprayed the agent with loose pea rock and inhaled the sweet scent of freedom, ahhhhh ... or was it that dang Pine thang. The unimpressive coconut border swept past.

Fakyah hadn't been pretending to be asleep. She actually slept through the episode, so they still didn't have many fond memories together.

"Wake up Fakyah, we're in the Keys now," Blu reported as the fiftieth, according to his count, Tiki bar whizzed by. A colorful hand written sign, propped against a dead coconut tree, read –SAFETY WARNING--LAST TIKI BAR FOR 1 MILE & I'M NOT KIDDING.

Meanwhile

A phone rang in Miami.

Pepto Ramirez, known as "El Gran Frijole" in the Mexican drug cartel, was an illegal gangster res-hiding in Miami.

Pepto and his Mexican bodyguard, Truman Chipotle, were holed up in a cheap one-room apartment at the Sweaty Palms Boatel, downtown near the Dick Dock Bar. They looked at each other over warm Pabst Blue Ribbon beers. "I'm loving deez Miami Beetch!" Pepto said. His body language indicated he was harboring a piñata in his stomach.

"Cheep" as Truman Chipotle's enemies called him, (he had no friends), had been body guarding the Big Bean for five years. Truman did the dirty work, Pepto made the monies.

The phone rang. Pepto grabbed the banana shaped receiver, punched the green button and pushed his greasy double chins apart to accommodate the faux-fruit. "Pepto-Bismol heah! ... He called himself Bismol but no one else would. Still, that's how he saw himself, cool and soothing.

"*Hay problema con el dinero?*" a voice on the phone hissed.

Pepto didn't see it coming; he'd somehow forgotten he owed *Bro* ten grand. He began to lose his grip as a cold, deep blue bubble of fear escaped his lips and a smaller, more urgent one worked its way down his left pant leg. There would be hell to pay. Still, Pepto pushed on. With nothing to lose, it's easy to gamble, but hard to find a game.

"Leeve with it!" Pepto screamed into the banana. The way Pepto said "IT," then, "You stinky person and smeller of taco wrappers!" left no doubt that he, El Gran Frijole, knew more about scaring the shit out of people, including himself, than most.

Truman Chipotle had been around the criminal element long enough to know what was going to happen. He pulled his gun and aimed it at Pepto's head. *I'll be damned if I'm 'going down' with this fat fuck,* he swore.

Pepto looked up, got scared, dropped the phone and, due to an untreated digestive problem, passed a most frightful trouser twister. Pepto called them "air theeners."

Truman could not bear another "air theener." He pinched his nose, turned the gun on himself and pulled the trigger. The gun jammed, but Truman Chipotle collapsed anyway and landed face first on the dirty, un-waxed terrazzo floor.

Two days later the Miami Beach police arrived at the Sweaty Palms after an anonymous caller reported something stinky in room 208. After briefly studying the bloated body, the chief medical examiner dashed to the window and hurled. Unfortunately, the window wouldn't open. It was an unpleasant few minutes. When he finally finished, the examiner stood up and noticed the unfired gun in Chipolte's hand. "Perhaps his demise was induced by the mere thought of shooting himself. It's not good for the heart and a particularly bad habit to get into," he opined and hurled again. The cops dragged Chipotle's body, ass first, from Room 2. It was easy; the floor was wet.

≈≈≈

Police looked for witnesses but Pepto was long gone, packed and pushing his recently stolen, candy-apple-red Chevy Camaro toward Key West, a well-known secret hiding spot.

Pepto made it to Key West in three hours and pulled up to the stop light on Flagler Avenue. The Camaro was immediately impaled by an old man on a Pogo stick. *"Conjo!"* Pepto screamed at the bouncing offender. His stolen golf clubs sprang forward and smacked him in the back of the head. "I keel you!" Pepto foamed at the fading geezer.

Pepto rented a room at the Organic Fruits Motel on Ben Dover lane and, having nothing else to do and wanting to stay in the game, made plans to get even with "El Gringo del Pogo."

Key West

Blu, Fakyah and the Ferd made it to Key West where they happily pissed Blu's four-hundred dollar winnings away. Blu tried to call his Uncle Bagwidth several times, but all he got was a message saying "It's a good day to die, don't bother leaving a message."

Blu and Fakyah holed up in the El Rauncho Motel for three nights. On day four, Blu was getting desperate for more cash. His thoughts turned to Bingo, but there were no games for "big players" like him, so he asked around about how to make a lot of money, quick. He met an indigent squatting near the algae-filled motel pool. The scruffy looking fellow was trying to catch tadpoles with a condom. "Lots of protein," the squatter said, popping one (tadpole) in his mouth. Blu squatted next to him, "Hey man, like how do you make some big money around here?"

"Bubba, like all I know is, that, like, there is some peoples an' like, they, like, ah, making the Meth and they making plenty big monies."

"Meth, huh?" Blu gave the guy two bucks and the guy gave Blu a condom filled with squiggling tads. Blu stretched the condom, tied a knot and twisted it to look like a wiener dog then let it snap back. He nodded at Captain Tadpole and took the stunned polliwogs back for Fakyah.

Fakyah was still asleep. Blu pushed her tongue in, put

the tads in a glass by the bed, saved the condom and left instructions for her.

He got directions to the library from an old woman out walking her turtle. At the library he looked up meth in a 1942 edition of Webster's dictionary. Down the M page he found methane. "Dang, that's what they must use to make meth out of," Blu thought. "OK, so now alls I gotta do is find me some methane, refine it and Wala! Meth." Blu liked the way the word meth slid off his tongue with a lisp. Am I gay? He wondered briefly and headed back to El Rauncho.

Blu stopped to steal a newspaper and talk to a city employee who was digging an inflatable love doll out of a storm drain on Truman Avenue near the Nasty Thang bookstore. "Hey, scuse' me bubba ahh... you know where there's any methane to be had?" Blu asked furtively.

"Conjo! Cuzzie there's a shit load of it out to Mount Trashmore," the worker replied. Blu had heard about Mount Trashmore while in Miami. It was the landmark city dump, located on Stark Island, not far from where Blu now stood. Influential locals hoped Donald Trump would buy the dump someday. It was also the location to which the Ohio turkey buzzards flocked every year, for a family reunion.

The city worker tugged again and the partially inflated doll popped out with a sucking sound. The sudden freedom activated the doll's *"sexy female"* voice feature. Laid out near the curb, the doll deflated slowly and croaked her last, and maybe first, static filled love words. "Give... It... to... Me... you... bi..." The battery died, so did the doll. The price sticker was still on it! Man, that's sad,

Blu thought and watched her soul ascend with a hiss.

≈ ≈ ≈

Back at the El Rauncho, Blu finished rolling a spliff with the front page of the "Mullet Wrapper," as the local newspaper was known. He made his hand into a fist, stuck the bone between two fingers, lit it and took a toke. A vanishing picture of someone named Farto smoldered near the smoking tip. "Focus, Blu!" he commanded himself and worked a well-worn flip-flop string between his aquiline toes.

He got up and unwound a coat hanger, to make it longer, then poked Fakyah with it. Fakyah, he knew, could be *touchy* after a nap. Blu poked her butt and whispered, "Fakyah, baby, we're out of money, so we're out of here. Let's go find us a place to live."

"Live?" Fakyah awoke instantly and delivered a perfectly executed *Chia ri* jab toward Blu's throat. She stopped short, paused and stretched. It made Blu dizzy. The stretch threw him off his game more than the punch would have. Blu embraced his weakness.

"Live and procreate ...?" Fakyah bleated and kept stretching her long spine. It crackled like Rice Krispies. She was long and knew it. While Fakyah cracked and packed, Blu cranked up the Furlane and drove to Stark Island where, with a silent prayer, he put a rock on the gas pedal, stepped back and plowed the Ferd deep into the mangroves across the street from the Key West Golf Course, near Hole #16. No one would find it there.

Blu walked back to the El Rauncho, gathered up Fakyah, grabbed some items from the room and together they took the bus to Stark Island. The outbound bus sign read - SOON - in faded orange letters. The driver looked puzzled when Blu strapped a king size mattress, a toilet seat and two lounge chairs onto the bike rack.

The couple de-bussed at the Cow Key Bridge, near the understated entrance to Key West. They followed beer cans and condoms to an encampment under the span and set up with all the stuff they borrowed from El Rauncho.

The first thing Blu did was grab a water-logged Gumbo Limbo branch from the shore line and insanely beat the shit out of a dead mullet floating nearby. He leaped in the air and screamed words he'd learned in Sunday school, Blu wanted to let the other shruburbian's to understand he was not one to be messed with.

After he established his turf, Blu offered to show the un-housed pilgrims his third nut as a sign of peace. There were no takers.

Blu fired off a roach and tried to figure out how to make meth. He had his own ideas.

≈≈≈

The next day, Blu refocused and headed toward Mount Trashmore. Fakyah stayed under the bridge and convinced a soil satchel to fan her with a palm frond while she ate the last of the sunbaked, free range, polliwogs with ketchup.

Mount Trashmore was composed of layers of dirt and garbage and had served as the city dump and incinerating facility for many years. It was also used by the Sheriff's department as a drop off point for confiscated marijuana bales. Most of the illegal herb was burned in the large, gas fired, incinerator. Tons of confiscated reefer arrived and clouds of white, pungent smoke could often be seen wafting from the incinerators' chimney during the burns.

During the wafting, the prevailing winds blew cloud after cloud of pot smoke across the mangroves and into the county jail. It took months before Sherriff, who resided in an air conditioned office, noticed that many of the inmates were spending more time than usual in the exercise yard and the guards generally seemed happier. It took several more months before he figured out why so many prisoners failed their drug test, even when they had no drugs.

Blu approached the base of the fertile mound. He stared at the sun then, with steely determination, began his ascent of the North Face of Mount Trashmore. Driving pitons made of Heineken bottles into the stinky mound, he reached the summit in less than twenty-minutes. He discovered a tattered *Cinzano* umbrella on the way up and planted it on the summit.

It was getting late and he was on the shadowy north face. Blu stood tall and claimed the territory for his own dang self. "The air just smells different up here," he said softly and inhaled the historic fumes. After a few moments of reflection, Blu began to build his meth lab by driving a scavenged pipe into the fertile soil. The sharp impact echoed across the dump. Blu vigorously smacked the pipe with an old bowling ball, driving the steel tube deep into the reeking mound. He hoped to extract the methane, which he would somehow (he hadn't figured that part out yet and had to go back to the library) convert into Meth.

"Man, it' gonna be great to be rich, rich as a bitch..." Blu thought and flicked his Bic to see better under the umbrella. *Kaboom!*

Immediately and involuntarily airborne, Blu's trajectory took him half way up to the buzzard's flight path and for a moment, a Golden Moment, Blu was free. "I'm Fr..." It was all he had time to say before gravity had its way and he returned to earth. He augured, face first, into the marl road near the base of the dump and wondered why anyone would do a drug like this. Beside him were two almost dead buzzards also augured, beak first, into the crushed coral surface. Their scraggly talons weakly clawed the dirt behind, as if trying to signal someone. The clawing Hinckley's didn't look too good; apparently they lost their thermals and became unable to stay aloft.

But, because the road was sloped like a ski run, the landing had been "Rough, but do-able," Blu later told Fakyah.

Blu was slightly injured upon impact and remained flat and motionless. He stared down his nose like a hypnotized chicken at the dirt in front of him He was confused and remembered drinking too much, a few nights before, at the Spooner Wharf Bar. The Spooner Wharf was an establishment where everyone shared a chair, a saloon where one customer sat down on the other. A place where frisky young gay people turned bar stools upside down and made a table for four. The last little bit of old Key West.

Blu knew he was drunk when everything began to make sense and the story Captain Buzz told the crowd of land-locked boozers that night made sense, even without drinking. Buzz told the tale of the Hinckley buzzards, a story about how he'd almost been killed by the stinky carrion birds. Blu remembered the smarmy crowd, all gathered up, asshole to elbow on the rickety Spooner dock. It was late and some of the older boozers started to tip over but most were fat enough to float so Buzz ignored them. Buzz stood in front of the gathered thongs and explained how the buzzards flew in from Hinckley, Ohio. How they winged a thousand miles south to poop on us, the taxpaying locals, at will. "They almost fuckin kilt me!" Captain Buzz was incensed by the memory, "Them fucking birds sometimes lose their thermals and crash. There is no excuse for that. They could kill someone." Buzz took a swig and continued, "I was on my sailboat up north of Key Tax Haven, it was real hot weather an' I seen buzzards flyin' overhead and offshore and like ...dang it Buzz! Wait a second, buzzards don't fly where they can't eat ... it was that quick in my mind, an' ...then ...fifteen of them fuckers dropped out of the sky and plowed into my boat. I got a picture! I was the only thing they could hope to land on. They tried. It didn't work. Talk about fast food, fuck, I had to go below to keep from getting speared by a freaking bird! ... None of em' made it... Sumbitches stink and don't have no respect for private property." Blu did not know what a thermal was at the time, but now, as he clawed his way upright, he was curious.

He recovered slowly, looked up from his landing zone and tried to taxi off the tarmac when he saw a pair of legs coming at him from the top of the dump. Behind the legs a metal contraption dragged through the fetid earth. Nice furrow for beans, Blu caught himself thinking.

"Howdy, young fella," the older man said.

" Harumph, gag, hack." Blu spit out a mouthful of pea rock.

"I heard a 'splosion and come a running...looks like you took a bad lick, son."

"Yup." Blu checked his components.

"Maybe you need some help... you know anybody in this town?"

"Nope, not really, only my old, fucked-up Uncle, Ferling Bagwidth."

"Bagwidth, eh? Dang it son...why...wait a minute, I'll be darned, that's me! I'm Ferling Bagwidth!"

"You're kidding?"

Bagwidth got excited and hit the ground with the Looner-Too. It ignited for the final time and shot skyward impaling a low flying Hinckley. The stricken bird plummeted to earth nearby.

"Dang Uncle, your message said not to leave a message so I dint." Blu offered.

"Just as well son, I hit a rough patch for a few years. That is until just a few minutes ago when I pre-fected that goddamn stick and now I'll be rich, big time rich! You brought me luck, son!"

"Wow," Blu said, "I could use some of that kind of luck."

"Hey, why don't you come back to my shop and we'll catch up on old times."

"Ah, OK, ah...where's your teeth, Uncle?'

"Left em' in the planter."

"Oh."

"Where's your ear, young fella?"

"I lost it in an apple bobbing contest at 4H."

"Oh."

Bagwidth pulled the Looner-Too out of the buzzard, the worn rubber tip made a sucking sound. The new-found relatives ambulated down the marl road and caught the bus heading back to town. Blu stopped the bus to pick up Fakyah under the Key Cow Bridge. Blu yelled over the rail, "Fakyah, get your ass up here!"

Bagwidth stood in front of the bus waving a bloody pogo stick to prevent the driver from pulling away. Like a scene from an old Tarzan movie, Fakyah appeared from underneath the bridge. An urban native trailed behind and carried her gear on his head. Other shruburbians waved goodbye to their queen. Fakyah was something else.

The trio boarded the bus and soon disembarked near Bagwidth's house on Dung Beetle Lane.

Fakyah's skin had a greenish tint. "Them tadpoles tasted funny," she burped. She pushed the front door open, scooped a pile of "How to cure toe nail fungus..." articles off the couch, curled up, did something that sounded like a frog croak and was asleep on the mildewed fabric within seconds. The tip of her pink tongue lolled between her lips. She cradled her sling backs to her chest.

"That's some woman, Blu."

"She needs rest," Blu said and pushed her tongue in.

≈≈≈

Bagwidth and Blu walked down to the Full Moon Saloon to reminisce. Ol' Leather Lips Langley, a local favorite, strangled the microphone with historic intent and belted out a forgotten country tune by Pine Top Perkins.

≈≈≈

It took Pepto a couple days to track Ferling Bagwidth down. He had a connection in the Miami sewer department. A guy who knew his shit. The connection gave Pepto the name of a guy in the Key West sewer department. "He knows his shit," the friend covertly advised.

Pepto met his source behind an old septic tank on Stink Bug Alley. A crisp twenty dollar bill appeared and Lenny "Honker" Sawyer provided information that led to Bagwidth.

"Old man Bagwidth lives down to Dung Beetle Lane, over to the cemetery. He's freaking nuts with that Pogo stick and shit," Honker advised.

Pepto knew that this guy "Bagwhatever" must be an asshole if he was into Pogo sticks. He looked again at the hood of his stolen Camaro and decided to leave a note on one of Bagwidth's neighbors' doors saying, "Any *persona* who wanting to keel Senor Bagwater-you calling me. I paying plenty big monies." He wrote the Organic Fruits Motel's phone booth number and signed the note, *El Gran Frijole.*

Pepto walked up Dung Beetle lane and saw a house with no front door. He walked up the steps and yelled into the house, "Hola!"

Fakyah got up and yawned. In front of her stood a fat Latin dude with small feet and a big diamond ring, "What's your name?" he asked.

"Fuck Ya!" she said, covertly eyeballing the ring. Her mouth remained open. Pepto liked her spirit.

"Fakyah?" he repeated. It sounded exotic and faraway. "You bet."

Pepto never had an A-rab before. "Si...let's do eet!"

Ten minutes later, Pepto left the house. He was stunned after a thorough and hearty pummeling. He remembered to breathe, but forgot to take the note or check his ring finger.

When Pepto departed, Blu and Bagwidth were taking a whiz in the bushes nearby. Pepto passed without noticing them. Suddenly Pepto stopped; he stared at his left hand, *"Conjo! My reeeng! My reeeng!"* He was afraid to go back. She'd almost killed him without using her hands just a few minutes ago. Still, Pepto continued to vent on his way down the lane. *"My reeng, my reeng."*

Blu and Bagwidth came home to find Fakyah squatting on the kitchen sink washing her private parts with a coconut soap infused loofa sponge and the rinse hose. It was on pulse. She stared at a new ring on her thumb.

Blu got an uncalled-for boner. He bent over, awkwardly, and picked up a piece of paper lying on the floor. Blu looked up. Fakyah looked down.

"Oh, ah, that Cuban guy must have dropped that when he came, I mean stopped, over, to check the, ah, junction box, ah..." Fakyah mumbled to a stop. She quickly changed frequencies and went to work with the loofa. Blu quickly figured out what happened and was a tad pissed-off. Fakyah noticed his moodiness and poked at Blu's trouser tent with a wet spatula. He forgave her and thought of the elderly Tinkerbelle, who probably hadn't forgiven him for stealing her car. It was good to be the first to forgive.

Blu took Bagwidth aside, "Hey Uncle Bag look at this, man! This guy Pepto wants to take out a hit on your ass."

Bagwidth looked at the note. "... a hit on my ass? Hot damn, that must be the fucking fuck-wad in the Camaro. He looked awful sensitive to me, on the way by."

Blu's mind began to turn.

"It says monies, and I need monies," Blu looked sideways at his uncle.

"Whoa!! Now hold on there, young fella! I ain't sure this is the best time for that thought. Look, I got monies too and I'm gonna get plenty more monies once that danged stick sells. How about this...ah... you take the contract on my ass... git some money up front and then don't kill me and we'll split it?"

"Well... I like it... but I see one problem...when Pepto finds out what I did I guess he'll want to kill me too," said Blu.

"Good point."

"Well, there's more than one way to grip a bowling ball!" Blu liked that one. He wasn't sure it was right, but he liked it. "How about I agree to kill you, get his monies, then you pay me with his monies, to kill him. Problem solved!"

"Let's Dewar!" Bagwidth said, with some relief. He poured them each a glass of his favorite scotch.

Killing was new to Blu. The only thing he had ever tried to kill was time, and he was already in jail when he did it.

All Blu had to do was make the hit without getting caught, but he worried. His time in jail had scarred him. He promised himself he would never go back to the Big House.

Blu laid awake and put ideas together like pieces of a shattered mirror. He would use his own life experience. But Blu had a bad memory and little experience. He fell asleep thinking about the two buzzards that hadn't been as lucky as he.

≈≈≈

The next morning, Blu headed for a phone booth. I

guess the first thing to do is set up a meet, he thought.

Fakyah walked him to the corner, pivoted and told Blu she was going into town to pawn the ring. She'd been a little pissy since eating those fermented tadpoles. Maybe she felt bad about what happened with Pepto.

"You know, Blu, when I was young I got into the habit of eating and I was hoping you had the same habit," she said and jumped into an empty seat on a passing Conch Train.

Although they had not yet found time or circumstance for a physical encounter, Blu was feeling some likings for Fak. He didn't want to lose her and anyway, it *was* a nice ring.

"I...eeeeeehh." Blu exhaled silently and watched Fakyah disappear in traffic.

≈ ≈ ≈

For some reason, Blu felt responsible for Fakyah and redoubled his thinking efforts. He went to a phone booth near the Spooner Wharf and discreetly slipped inside. He thumbed a few coins into the slot, shifted onto his left foot and inadvertently crushed a large palmetto bug with his flip flop. Blu dialed the number with a bony forefinger. It was the number that would change his life.

Busy.

Blu tried again. After twenty rings, "Si?"

Unfortunately, when Pepto answered, Blu was bent over, balancing on one foot trying to scrape the quarter-pound bug off his flip-flop. He saw the words Fuk Yoo written upside down in red lipstick on a panel near the floor. He dropped the receiver he'd been holding between his neck and shoulder. It swung down on its cord, bounced off the glass and hit Blu in the front teeth. "I'm going to kill every one of you fuckers!" Blu screamed at the offending bug. He quickly recovered his composure and grabbed the dangling receiver.

Pepto overheard everything and liked this guy's style.

"Si?" Pepto said again.

'Yo man it's me, the guy who wants to take out Old Bagwater. I'm a pro and can gitt'er done. My name's Yellow." Blu knew better than to give his real name, or mention Fakyah.

"Jello?"

"No, listen man, I'm not hungry and I can hear you good. What kind of monies are we talking about, Seen-your Pepto?"

"Monies?"

"You know, to knock off Bagwater."

"Oh conjo! You finding dee note, man. Is berry good for me. Eet was making me to have nervousnesses. Maybe you finding beeg ring too? Sí? No?"

"Let's talk monies, like how much?" asked Blu.

"Jel-low?"

"I can hear you man, go ahead..."

"I'm thinking like four-hundred beans for taking out the Bag," Pepto piped.

That's not a lot of money for not doing anything Blu thought, understanding full well that two negatives can, in certain cases, make a positive. And, it was money. But what if he had to pay income tax on it someday? Blu knew he could outsmart this crook, "Four hundred fifty plus tax that makes it four hundred eighty three dollars and seventy five cents. Half now and half when it's done," Blu knew how to bargain.

"Half of four hundred eighty-three dollars and seventy five centavos eez ... ah ... ah ... that's *mucho* beans for one bullet. You gonna use a gun right?"

"Sure and a calculator and it ain't a lot for a pro job, neither." Blu tried to sound backwoods dumb. He succeeded and was excited by his accomplishment.

"You take food stamps?"

"Cash ... and change."

"Then we got deal?" Pepto felt somewhat relieved that things had been so easy.

"Deal. Meet me at the Red Squid in one hour. Bring the cash ... and change; I'll be wearing a Frog Breath T-shirt. Do you need a receipt?"

"No, but, to make meetings of crime in *El Calamari Roja?* Maybe eez not so good to do, No, sí ... eh?"

"Hasta linguini," Blu said, also relieved that things had been so easy. Blu needed transportation. He walked back to the Spooner Wharf and stood out front. Within minutes a likely candidate rode past on a bike. Blu jumped out and screamed, "Hey dirt bag, that's MY bike!" The frightened shruburbian dropped the bike and ran into bushes. Blu smiled and peddled home with a warm, felonious, wind at his back.

Blu decided to his change his appearance for the gig, in case things went south. Wait a minute; things can't go any farther south than Key West. Anyway, he needed a good disguise and it had to work. He found some of Fakyah's pubic hairs in an ash tray. Methodically, he glued them to his chin and upper lip. He put a couple in each ear and nostril just to be safe. Blu got some residue from his bong and did his eyes. A final wrapping of a polyester sarong and fake coconut tits should do the trick. He'd look like a local.

At 4:00 p.m. Blu arrived at the Red Squid, a subtropical titty-bar just off Grovelers Lane at four o'clock. He spotted a red Camaro, fitting Uncle Bag's description, in the parking lot. A dent in the hood and a set of golf clubs in the back confirmed his suspicion.

Blu opened the outer door and entered a cubic space that was, "Dark as a well-digger's ass." (Blu was glad he wasn't the one who confirmed this time-honored analogy.) The sudden daylight had the effect of a large flashbulb going off. Panicked faces were frozen in a pure white and heavenly light. The local politicos didn't perceive the light as heavenly and frantically covered their well-known faces and or crotches. Everyone saw dancing white spots and quick decisions, for which Key West politicians are known, were made. The door hissed shut. Two dimly lit arrow signs flashed. SQUIDS flashed in red and pointed left, the other flashed GEEZER'S, in white, and pointed back toward the front door. Blu did not consider himself a geezer and slipped into the smunky room. The awe-inspiring vinyl-scented booths smelled like the long dead love doll. A vaporous tincture of chlorine, cum, money and rum was the night's perfume. He sidled over to a dark curtained corner and plopped down in a booth to wait. It felt lumpy but soft.

"*CONJO!*" bellowed a fat Latin man, quickly zipping his fly. "*Mang*, you crazy? What kind of bitch are you?"

Blu was startled, but quickly recognized Pepto's voice.

"Chill out, its how I work," Blu said, still sitting in

Pepto's lap.

"Oh, OK... Jew Jello?"

"OK, enough with the greetings. I'm a Lutheran. Where's El Dinero, los monies?

"Dinero?"

"Sí, el dinero for making bang-bang on Bagwater, amigo!"

Pepto didn't feel comfortable, *"Conjo!"* he mumbled and pushed Blu off his lap. A fat envelope slipped out of his guayubera. "Make eet queeek!" he said too loudly.

The local crotch watchers turned toward them like sharks to a wounded Hawaiian. The envelope dropped to the floor and four hundred-dollar bills fell out between Pepto's legs. Blu bent over to grab the bills. One of the dancers noticed. Exotic dancers can see money like a moth can see a flame. She shook her head sadly as Blu walked toward the exit. Was the well-formed female ass losing value, like the dollar?

≈≈≈

Blu walked into his uncle's house to find Fakyah sitting in a yellow plastic kayak, a bag of groceries between her legs. "Look, Blu, we got food, an' I got my own bed."

Blu grabbed a fresh Twinkie, "Where's the paddle?"

"What paddle?" she said.

It just didn't seem right anymore. He got a meek boner, but the bloom was off on the rose. Blu shook his head and walked away to think and nap. He napped.

Blu snapped awake with a full understanding of the situation and what to do about it. He didn't know how he knew, but he knew he knew. "He knew, he knew, he knew," Blu said the words again, thirty-nine times to be exact. He carefully pronounced the K each time.

The clock was ticking.

Blu quickly figured that Fakyah intended to pork the Cuban again, for purely gastronomical reasons, of course.

Let's play this one first, Blu thought. He began feeding Fakyah false information. He knew she would pass it on to Pepto.

"Fakyah, I, ah, took me a job to pop that Cuban guy who wrote the note. So I need to catch him in a **crowded place**, a place where there are lots of people."

"He's going to be pissed."

"Not for long."

≈≈≈

As Blu predicted, Pepto showed up on Dung Beetle Lane a few days later. Fakyah took another ring off him then told him about Blu. It's for Blu's own good, she explained to herself. She didn't want Blu to go away. She had some likings for him, too.

Blu lurked in the bushes and thought he heard several muffled queefs. He waited until the kayak stopped squeaking. Finally, Pepto slipped out the doorway, like a wet fish from a plastic bag, and headed down Dung Beetle Lane.

Blu went in the house and grabbed a Key Deer beer. He walked over and handed Fakyah a pass, purchased with Bagwidth's money, for a round of golf at the Key West Golf Hole Course and Mosquito Boutique. The ticket was for the last nine holes and dated for the coming Wednesday.

"Hey, Fak, I found this golf ticket out on the street, why don't you go play golf, I'm going to take a few days off

and go walk about."
"Walk about what?"
"Just things."
"Okay. I'm hungry."

Blu knew Fakyah had a conscience and would give the golf pass to Pepto to make herself feel better about the rings.

With the plan initiated, Blu headed for Stark Island.

≈ ≈ ≈

The old Furlane was still mushed into the mangroves and Blu set about making an FOB (forward operating base.) During the next three nights he scavenged the Key West Golf Hole Club fairways for golf balls, but only the old ones. The Golf Hole Club was a well-manicured swamp and formal burial ground for old golf balls. "The old ones are slow and easily hunted," his mom used to say about her ex-husbands. And, anyway, the new ones wouldn't work; they had to be the old kind, made out of rubber bands. Working day and night he unstrung the geriatric balls. In the mangroves near the Ford, he stretched the wrinkled rubber back and forth between two Gumbo Limbo trees. The sling was over forty feet long. The Fairlane was ass out twenty feet back in the mangroves and centered on the sling.

Later, Blu rifled through the dumpsters behind the jail and found an old body bag the tag read - B. FARTO. The bag was stuffed with Cuban coffee sacks, a short red cocktail dress and six pairs of red socks, made into hand puppets.

Blu fashioned the top portion of the body bag into a hat to keep the mosquitoes off his head. The bottom portion was secured to the elongated rubber band with a pair of pretty nice Nike shoe laces he borrowed from a sleeping pilgrim.

Up before Wednesday's dawn, Blu had one last mission to complete. He needed ammo, one round. The tropic sun came up like an old lava lamp glob as Blu searched the lonely dump, hoping for an easy pick. He looked for his old landing groove in the dirt. The painful furrow was gone, but the memory remained.

Time was running out. He settled for the freshest dead buzzard he could find. "This one's still got some good rigger-mortis," Blu mumbled as he departed the base of Mount Trashmore. He dragged the buzzard downhill and named it Three, since the numbers One and Two had been retired.

The plan was beginning to take shape. Blu knew Pepto could not resist a free golf pass and would feel safe on the golf course. "No crowds," Fakyah would remind him.

Blu also knew Pepto would sport his gold jewelry to impress the beer girl. She would counsel him, "Gee, *Senor*, the weight of all that gold could affect your swing, I will hold it for you, if you like." There could be an unexpected bonus in my future, Blu conjured and calculated that Pepto would tee-up on Hole 16 about eight-thirty Wednesday morning. He was excited. It's always exciting when you don't know if you're going to screw up or not.

Blu rigged a piece of hemp line and a scavenged come-along to the rear bumper of the Ford. Three was rigged in the body bag. "Just like David and Goliath, an' sorta like Robin Hood..." Blu laughed and envisioned Robin Hood running through Nottingham Forest with dead buzzards sticking out of his quiver.

Who would ever know; who would ever figure it out? The perfect crime! "Blu, you good, you just plain good, man," he mumbled and swatted a skeeter.

"Just bad luck," some pundits would say. "Maybe it was them thermals," those without knowledge would quip and not recognize they were accidently right, for once in their life.

At zero-eight-thirty Pepto teed up on Hole 16, just as Blu calculated.

Blu squatted in the bushes and watched.

Pepto stood, legs apart, at least at the ankles, swinging his fat butt back and forth like a three hundred pound Muscovite duck.

"Like that's gonna save him." Blu mumbled and cranked back on the giant rubber band. It was now or never, the final countdown. Earlier that morning, Blu packed Three, ass-first, into the body bag and now, at the final moment and full tension, Blu stepped in front of the launch module to re-check Three's aerodynamics. Blu did not notice a large iguana chewing on the oily, but tasty, hemp restraining cord.

Blu stepped back to admire his work and began to initiate the launch sequence in his mind.

Pepto tee'd up.

The iguana took its final bite.

Blu was airborne. He was out in front with the buzzard an uncomfortably close second. Nose and beak they flew across College Road. Blu tried to outthink the dead buzzard and grabbed Pepto by the alligator emblem on his golf shirt on the way past. They tumbled to the ground.

The buzzard sailed harmlessly overhead and embedded, beak first, in a stunted Malayan palm. Pepto rolled over and dug a Whopper-sized divot out of his mouth. Two golfers, waiting for the tee, dialed 911 and ran toward them to help.

"I've never seen anything quite like it," one white-haired duffer said to the newspaper photographer who showed up a few minutes later.

"That guy," the other duffer pointed at Blu with his putter, "came out of nowhere and saved the gentleman in front of us. Quite remarkable!"

"I not finding my balls," Pepto said weakly, tripping on the divot left by Blu's ass.

Blu came out of his velocity-induced haze in time to hear someone say to Scooter O'Neal, the crime scene photographer, "That man's a hero!" O'Neal pulled Blu's wallet out and looked at his ID. "This man's name is Blu Yunger."

Blu passed out as the flash went off.

"That won't work, sweetie," Scooter said to Scoop O'Haskins, the local paramedic and crime reporter. Scoop and Scooter eyeballed the scene. "Needs more light, some sun. Be a bunny and turn him around, twist his head up more," Scooter ordered. Scoop grabbed Blu's ankles and spun him around. He cocked Blu's tousled head and set it on a red ladies' tee marker made out of a painted coconut. "Needs more character Pooky, more feeel ..." Scooter said, checking his own hair in the view finder then focusing the camera on Blu's inert body. "Oh my, let's see; let's put some dirty dirt on that cut near his left eye, smear it...smear it...OH, my! Yes! and push his tongue in, Bunny

Butt... that will help balance the shot ... just love the red hair, it brings out the blood ... yes, oh yes."

"Just hold your pooter, Scooter!" said Scoop, who worked part time at the Ate-O-One bar. With a certain Irish charm Scoop O'Haskins pulled out his industrial make-up kit and quickly made Blu look good, too good. Blu awoke to see his distorted face in a close-up lens and heard Scooter O'Neal say, "Hold that look! Oh! It's good, it's Good, hold, hold, hold..." the flash went off just as Blu coughed up some turf and ruined the shot. "Leave me the fuck alone!"

"Well..." huffed Scooter, "You Big Strapper, you. YOU could have been someone, someone ...big, really big."

"Yeah, someone really big, Mister BLU Yunger," echoed O'Haskins.

Pepto was both puzzled and concerned by the attention focused on this guy named Blu Yunger. He watched as Three lost rigor and, beak still embedded, folded down alongside the coconut trunk like a piece of wet macramé. "I having deeze feeling too..." he mumbled.

There was something familiar about the guy who saved him, but Pepto couldn't put his finger on it. Then, in an epiphanic moment, Pepto recognized Yellow. Blu was Yellow. Pepto knew that blue and yellow mixed together made green and that's what he was truly after, some green! Some big green. He admired Blu's-Yellow's style and, as a professional courtesy, refrained from asking why *Senor* Bagwidth was still alive. It was time to form an alliance. With Blu's fame, Pepto's brain, Fakyah's ass and Bagwater's ... ah ... anyway, he could gain control of this dumb little island and make some real green.

Pepto gave Blu a ride home from the golf course and avoided looking at the dimple in the hood. They arrived at Bagwidth's to find Beth asleep in the kayak. Ferling was on the porch watering his herbs and, after uncomfortable introductions, veiled threats, a pooling of weapons and apologies for previous relationships and misunderstandings, it was decided by Blu, Bagwidth and Pepto that "Team Fakyah" would be formed to run "Miss Fakyah" for Mayor of Key West. Someone should tell her, they all agreed, and waited for her to wake up. She smiled coyly when informed.

Maybe "It" just started, Blu thought the next day when he saw his inked face on the front page of the daily newspaper, the Mullet Wrapper. His eyes looked like Elizabeth Taylor's and his cheeks looked red even in black and white. The word HERO was smeared across the front page in big black type face. "Local indigent saves fat dude on golf hole." "Dead buzzard sent to Miami for questioning." "Meet *'Buzzard Boy'* at Flaming Maggie's bookstore this Wednesday."

They put the plan in motion.

≈≈≈

Determined to win the mayoral election for Fakyah and coasting on his new-found notoriety, Blu took Fakyah to all the self help gatherings and AA meetings in town. Among others, they attended the Adult Children of Old Boozers, Overeaters Synonymous, Free Prostate screenings, the Stop Smoking or I'll Kick Your Ass martial arts center and support group, the Mean People Against Chickens Society and the Sex, Love and Oyster Eater Addicts Anonymous. There were a lot of groups. In fact, their members made up the city's largest voting bloc. She also made a clandestine appearance amongst a small group of very nervous people who gathered in an undisclosed location to admit a dirty little secret-they all lived in Key West and, none of them were writing a book! Fakyah thought it was sad.

Blu also took Fakyah up US Highway 1 as far as Big Copout Key. She always drew a crowd and looked good during her appearances. Blu bought her a portable 100 psi air compressor to use on stage and fashioned a custom air -nozzle out of a Budweiser beer can. He covered the can with a coolie cup to prevent injury. Fakyah just loved it. Everywhere she went her breasts bubbered and crowds swarmed chanting, "FAKYAH! FAKYAH! GOOOOO-FAKYAH !"

Fakyah never spoke a word. It was better that way. But she had style and made Bagwidth, Blu and Pepto carry her around the campaign trail in her kayak. The locals loved it. Campaign signs, printed in large blue Lucida Face font on re-cycled condom boxes appeared all around town, "Fakyah-It's time for a Strange!"

≈≈≈

November came quickly. Winter was on the way and the temperature dropped one degree. Fakyah was tied in the polls.

The Mullet Wrapper's "Condensed Polls" showed –
In favor of Fakyah -1%
Opposed to Fakyah-1%
Undecided-98%
It was going to be close.
Hurricane season was almost over when the first

tropical depression was spotted, low crawling across the Atlantic. It slowly gained strength and was named *Areola*.

≈≈≈

"We've got to move forward, we vote on November sixth," Bagwidth said during their first campaign meeting.

"Where is that?" Fakyah asked.

"What?"

"Forward."

"You know, forward, like when you say something that sounds good, like...let's move forward on this issue."

"I can't say all that shit."

"Well you got to if you want to be a politician."

"Oh fuck. What if I don't? What kind of party are we anyway?" Fakyah squawked like a parrot.

"There are only two parties I know of," said Blu, "smokers and non-smokers." They quickly formed a quorum and fired off a bone.

On November third, tropical storm *Areola* breasted the Windward Islands and bore down on Key West with a vengeance. She grew larger and formed a perfect pink circle with a dark red eye on the NOAA color radar and, at one point, was classified as a 44 double-D storm. The image was eventually taken off the air by a federally mandated porn filter, but it was too late for some local weathophiles who were subsequently arrested for whacking-off every time the wind exceeded 25 knots, or the wet bulb dip ... never mind.

For whatever reason, the Weather Channel saw a sharp uptick in male viewers as *Areola* approached the Keys. The "Cone of Uncertainty" had puckered to the "Nipple of- Oh, No!" Residents were asked to evacuate the island but only those who couldn't afford to did. The voting precincts remained open since the people in charge evacuated early and forgot to cancel the election. The polling places were manned by patriotic gays, stalwart defenders of personal freedom and lubricant. They showed up in sunglasses, colorful snorkels, custom thongs and pledged to keep the booths open for the scheduled election. A young Japanese contingent, stranded on the island, promised to stand their ground on "E-rection Day," as they pronounced it, and readied their handmade bamboo voting booths.

Areola rapidly stiffened and clutched Key West to her bosom on November 6, Election Day.

Fakyah voted for herself, grabbed her kayak and headed for higher ground. Blu stayed, until the polls closed early, after three feet of seawater rushed in and the voting machines started to float and explode. The storm passed quickly.

Only twenty-nine handwritten ballots survived the electoral melee. Of those twenty-nine, eighteen were for Fakyah, five for Bum Farto and six for an unknown named Mike Sweeny. Sweeny called for a recount but was ignored. Fakyah was in. Mike Sweeny was out. Blu headed to the gala victory celebration to be held on high ground near Dog Beach. When he arrived, the beach was underwater and only a few people showed up. Unfortunately they were floaters, not voters. Fakyah was not among them.

Fakyah was gone when Blu returned to Dung Beetle Lane later that night. Her kayak was still in place, three packets of blonde hair dye laid open in the bottom. She'd left a hastily scribbled note, written in lipstick on a used

Taco Bell wrapper.

> *"Pepto got me, I gotta eat!!!*
>
> *Fakyah*
>
> *P.S. My real name is Beth. Really."*

≈≈≈

The following day, the Supervisor of Elections, in an attempt to explain the low voter turnout reported, "The stray 220 Volt Alternating Current combined with floating voting booths and smelly debris may have influenced some of the electorate." Both political parties immediately blamed the other.

The old conch house seemed unusually quiet to Blu, especially after saying *Beth* too many times, twenty-seven times actually. Blu wondered again about his strange ways. He said *Beth* slowly, seven more times. He still didn't know why. "That's thirty-four times I've said Beth. She told me her name was Fakyah?"

Blu mumbled to himself and walked into the kitchen. He rummaged through the cheese drawer in hopes of a sign. What does "Pepto got me," mean? He was pissed at Fakyah for leaving and not telling him her name was Beth but he didn't blame her. "That's the kind of life we live," he muttered. Still, she was the first woman he'd almost ever loved.

Folded neatly under the sharp, molting cheddar, he was shocked to discovered a note from his uncle.

"Deer Bl, Blu, I am gone too DC an over to the Pentagram they's interested in 'Looner-Too.' If I git rich I'll let ya know. Ferling- soon to be rich ... rich as a bitch- Bagwidth."

Blu glanced around the old house, looked at Fakyah's note and packed his things. He was upset and slammed the front door to punctuate his mood. He forgot there was no door and tumbled back into the house. With a deep sigh and a shake of his head, Blu dusted himself and caught a bus for Miami. Screw'em, he thought. He would return to the old ways. "I'm sick of everybody, 'cept me." Blu mumbled.

A Short Legend

For a few days Blu Yunger became a short-lived legend in Coconut Grove. At first, folks stood in line for hours to see his "Additional Member" and be regaled with a romantic story that always began, "Fakyah folks... she's real, I was there long enough to know." But the days passed and Blu, shrunken by loneliness, couldn't keep the act together. Then one ball tucked up and went on strike, but Blu didn't care. He was in another kind of love, the fervent love of that which you cannot possess.

≈≈≈

Time, wind and neutrinos passed through Blu. He could not give up the good life, or at least the thought of the good life. He set to thinking about "It" again. It, the thing that happens and you don't notice until later. It, the thing that changes everything. Blu hoped he wouldn't miss It. He needed a plan that would make him famous. "I miss that dang fame, gol' darnnit." He cried in his sleep and often awoke to find himself twisted in the sheets from trying to bone fish in his dreams.

≈≈≈

One afternoon a mighty thirst came upon Blu. "Lord, I'm dryer than a popcorn fart," his mom used to say in Latin when they went to church. His thirsty mom was always first in line for the wine at the Communion rail. The old people learned to let her through without a fuss.

Blu was broke and stopped at a local pet shop, Miami Mice. He skipped past the sullen rodents and went to the back of the store where he shook all the bird cages. The commotion set off a squawking roar of domesticated fowl. The attendant rushed up the aisle while Blu slipped behind a stack of kitty litter bags. Craftily, he made his way toward the front door, stopping to steal some change out of a Society for the Prevention of Cruelty to Animals jar. He *was* thirsty. He snatched up a pamphlet for camouflage and soon wrapped it around a cold "Key Deer Beer" purchased from a nearby 18 store. Blu loved the math, 7-11 ... duh! When the beer was gone, Blu read smeared words on the pamphlet that smelled like hamster litter. The pamphlet described the use of implanted micro-chips in dogs and cats. Put one on their ass and they can be tracked anywhere. He wished he'd implanted one on Fakyah's ass. Blu missed her and wondered if he should help her somehow.

On his own, he had to start thinking. It hurt.

≈≈≈

For a few days Blu moved in with a deaf, blind and mute older lady who lived near Miami Beach. The name on the mail box read, Mrs. Clover Greveland. Mrs. Greveland lived alone in a nice beachside cabana. She was awarded the house and some heavy cash when she divorced her husband, Bobby D. Greveland, some years before. Bobby D. spent his entire life trying to become famous in the country and western music world. Finally at age fifty, he made a lot of money with his # 2 country hit called, "Who's going to suck my dick when you're gone?" It didn't sit well with Clover. She filed and, although she prevailed

74

in court, Clover was ordered by Judge Winston Hummer to publically admit that the song did have a "Catchy refrain." It may have soured her.

Blu followed Mrs. Greveland into her large wooden beach house one day after she stepped out to get the newspaper on her porch, the porch where he'd been sleeping. He was hungry. She didn't seem to notice him. She didn't speak or turn, even when Blu, like Baby Dionysius, passed a "gassy omen." What do they call people who can't smell? Blu wondered. He assumed the best and was pretty sure she didn't know he was there. The rooms were large and colorful. He was very careful and very quiet and ate only left-over's. He did his business out back and, most importantly, was gone before the care-giver arrived every day at noon.

On those lonely days, Blu walked to the beach, pushed a drunk off a bench and watched old and young folks alike walk their pets. The beach was a dog doo minefield. He always marveled at how much folks do love their stinky little critters. Everybody needs love, and food and every kind of hungry dog passed his bench. Most of them were edible, Blu noted, although he was not fond of beagle.

"If you ain't had a buzzard," Blu gumped, "you ain't had shit!" He fondly remembered the two Hinckley's augured in next to him at Mount Trashmore, Old One and Two. Them buzzards were like friends, Dang! An' just like me, they caught a bad draft.

On this day Blu needed company. He needed a pet and glanced at a smelly drunk, face down, in the poo-pocked sand. A fat blue-bottle-blowfly landed on the inebriated one and, faster than a blur, Blu reached out and

75

snatched it. He quickly pulled its wings off and watched the fly stagger around on the back of his hand. Blu could see the little stubs flailing at two-hundred flaps per second. The fly gave Blu a universally understood look with a thousand pissed off eyes.

The beach and its obnoxiously happy people did not make Blu feel any better. But, he had a pet. He put on his game face and headed back to Greveland's. Still, during the walk home, he couldn't help but wonder if the old lady would notice his new pet.

Blu approached the house. He was almost sure the old lady was deaf. Carefully, he opened the creaking door and stepped inside. Instantly a violent smack on the back of his hand transformed the fly into a dozen pieces.

"It ain't enough I put up with your damn ass slinking around here all the time, but you ain't bringing no goddamned fly into this house. That's where I draws the line!" She brandished an old flyswatter and took another swing. Blu moved his hand and heard a whooshing sound. She missed but she was quick, Blu noted.

Blu was stunned. "I thought you was blind and deaf and shit."

"Do I look like I'm blind and deaf, you fuck-wad? I just tell people that so they'll leave me the hell alone. Why do you think I let you stay? It's cuz you don't say nothing. Do you think I pick up that damned newspaper every day just to wipe my ass, you dill pickled Nimrod?"

"Nimrod? Ah...well...what about the nurse who comes?"

"She's my sister and works for the county attorney, we got a thing going...she brings me dynamite reefer...don't fuck it up!"

"Yes, ma'am."

The fly was gone but Blu liked the old girl. She was spunky and reminded him of Fakyah...ah...Beth.

" And, by the way, where is your freaking ear?"

Ms. Clover Greveland had been young once, maybe twice, and during those days she captured a large percentage of the penises she desired. However, as time passed Clover became increasingly reluctant to use the "P" word. Life was a little "closer to the bone" in many respects and she cut corners where she could.

Time had taken its toll on Clover. She lived alone, or had lived alone, until this dipstick Blu moved in. The adrenalin-packed action with the flyswatter had excited her and it was time again, she thought, for the "P" word to be employed. She always fell for guys who were dumber than her and this guy was a real prize. She'd just won the Numb Skull lottery, "...and I kin' use a good roll in the hay," she mumbled and headed for the kitchen to "freshen up."

Blu crawled around on the floor recovering as many parts of his pet as possible. He spotted a bag of herb on a dining room chair near Clover's purse. He got up, put the fly parts in an ashtray and sat at the dining room table, hoping to have lunch or at least fire off a primo bone. Clover Greveland came out of the kitchen. She was naked under her colorful polyester house dress. She jumped in front of Blu, planted her feet, pulled her dress up and ruffled her muff. "Super Sex!" she cried.

"I'll take the soup," Blu said.

Hooboy, I got me a real winner here! Clover thought.

She returned to the kitchen and grabbed a condom out of the freezer and a bottle of Safflower oil from the cupboard. Blu saw her coming back. He grabbed the old lady's wallet, her stash and bailed.

Blu caught a westbound Greyhound and headed for the Emerald Coast.

≈ ≈ ≈

Twelve hours later, on Canibel Island, Blu awoke from a tequila-soaked dream. He arrived at the seashore the night before, where rainfall quickly ruined a beachside wedding celebration. Blu traded the damp bartender a couple of Clover's primo buds for all the leftover Tequila drinks.

Now, in the early morning light, Blu's face hurt. The last thing he remembered was eating hermit crabs at the high tide line, saying Beth thirty-nine times in a row and finishing the fifteenth Margarita. He was about to be in Margarita ill.

For awhile, he lay half awake and marveled at the natural world, so eternally temporary. He thought he saw Uranus in the morning sky. "Is that Uranus?" Blu mumbled and laughed at the impossibility of the statement.

But now, covered in sand, surrounded by little paper umbrellas and crumpled lime carcasses, Blu was awake and thirsty. He smelled the scent of a distant bush and started to get up. A strong hand held him down.

"Just take it easy son," said an authoritative voice from above. Blu rubbed finely ground crustaceans from his eyes and looked up to find a National Park Service ranger standing above him, hand on his gun. "Looks' like we got us a sit-u-ation here," the ranger said pointing at Blu's crotch with his trigger finger.

Am I back in Key West already? He felt a movement near his groined intersection and looked down to find a thirty-pound turtle nestled between his legs. The turtle pulled slowly and deliberately at the damp granules, its front flippers flopped as it burrowed under Blu's ass, digging deeper by the second. Sand ridden snot vented into the atmosphere in front of Blu's face.

"This here's a gen-u-wine fertile sea turtle." The ranger pointed at the turtle's almost vertical shell, "Come to shore to lay her eggs on the planet, son, an...well... looks like she picked your crotch to do it in."

Blu started to protest but the ranger, Officer Yasily Jercoff, according to his name tag, put his right hand on top of Blu's head, again. He skillfully handed Blu a page torn out of the Federal Park regulation manual with his left hand. Highlighted in yellow, *"No one, for any reason, shall willfully disturb the nesting grounds of the endangered sea turtle. Failure to observe this law may result in a fine of five thousand dollars and or imprisonment for a period not to exceed ten turtle years."*

Blu rounded up the last of his saliva, licked the page and stuck it on his forehead to keep the sun off his eyes. He stopped resisting and tried to be reasonable. We are all controlled by unreasonable people he thought; if it wasn't for those folks fucking things up we wouldn't need so many laws and rules. The thought evaporated. His thirst did not. He said so and within minutes a well- designed female ranger sporting a US Marine flat top hair cut brought him a bottle of chilled Evian and a breath mint.

With a quick and graceless maneuver, Blu stuffed the mint in the turtle's butt. In Blu's opinion the turtle needed the mint more than he did. He was being held prisoner by a dang turtle! Blu drank the water. It helped.

Without warning, the vertical turtle squawked and vented the mint fifteen-feet into the air where it was snatched by a circling gull that instantly plummeted, ass first, into the calm sea. The bird did not come up; the mint floated away. Nature can be a meanie. Blu did not know what to do next. He had a limited repertoire of proven moves.

Blu Yunger remained half buried in flying sand and endured a subterranean infringement that might have irritated a weaker or less lonely man. His hangover passed and he got hungry. He said so and again, within minutes, the well apportioned ranger returned with a pizza. Dang! Blu thought.

"Mushrooms and olives," she said as she leaned over and gave Blu a good view of her badge area. Her name tag read Tess.

"No onions?" Blu wise-cracked. In minutes he had onions and, as the sun began to set, the light began to dawn on Blu's horizon. "I get it," he whispered to the turtle's butt. Blu gazed at the winsome sky. He found his favorite planet and named the burrowing turtle after it. He also contemplated the exact meaning of the Law and reviewed the legal wording carefully by re-reading the page, still pasted upside down on his forehead. It was one of his talents.

Blu concluded that anyone who disturbed Him would also disturb the Turtle and therefore be equally guilty under the law. They would be charged with being an accessory to... disturbing a butt nest. Hum?

"I need a haircut. If I sneeze from all the sand in my hair it might spook the turtle," he told Tess, the shapely ranger. Tess ran to a nearby phone booth and dialed her barber. Jercoff told Blu that TV crews would be showing up the next day.

After resting his head in the lovely ranger's lap for four hours, the shift changed and Blu sported a fresh US Marine style flat-top hair cut. He decided to take a rain check on Officer Jercoff's proffered lap. He got to know the rangers pretty well as they ran back and forth serving his every demand. It was a strange fun and, as the sun blurped out of the sea like a fart in a bathtub, Blu admired his new finger and toenail polish, it was *Sea Turtle Green*.

After finding out about his possible TV appearance, Blu forked over some of Clover's cash and had the local Lee Nails girls brought in during the night. The girls painted Blu's digits while Tess's gay barber, named Sosoon, cut his hair. Blu remembered the Lee Nail girls fondly, the way they excavated his toes and held tiny flashlights in their perfect white teeth. The girls laughed softly and with compassion but the beams of light remained perfectly still. Blu almost sprang a boner but didn't want to get any more emotionally involved with the turtle than necessary. The laws of nature and National Geographic articles notwithstanding, Mama Turtle failed to lay her eggs the first night. She kept digging her nest and Blu suffered a major groin infringement when the turtle came up for air.

TV crews arrived early on the second day and set up their equipment. Blu was glad he spent the money and spiffed up but, was disappointed when he saw most of the cameras were focused on his crotch and the turtle therein. His sandy groin was on the Early Admission, a TV news show out of Miami. Blu held his breath when they manually zoomed in for a close up.

"Man gives birth to turtle, photos at eleven," was the teaser.

The reporters never asked Blu for his name. But when they asked Jercoff the turtle's name, the officer was momentarily silenced by the bright light of fame. Before Jercoff could bring himself to speak, Blu put both thumbs up and blurted, "Its URANUS!" Some looked up, some looked down. It was awkward.

Blu laughed to break the tension and tried to get his face in front of the camera but a pissed-off Jercoff held him by his short hairs with a small utility tool and threatened to pour sand in his mouth if he tried to speak again. Blu knew he was real close to famous and, he knew the definition of famous, "It's how many people know your name."

Blu tried to signal the TV crew with an SOS by passing wind at the required intervals. ... --- ... ... --- ... however, his signaling device was buried deep in the Gold Coast sand. The pulverized and unsympathetic crustaceans muffled the noise, but mama turtle began to stir.

"Don't frack the turtles," Jercoff counseled, using an old natural gas term that was unfamiliar to Blu, although natural gas was not.

A TV news helicopter suddenly hovered overhead,

blowing shit everywhere. The female ranger instinctively plummeted face first into Blu's crotch and frantically brushed sand over the nest. Blu lost focus and stared at the top of her brush-cut while trained professional, Y. Jercoff, pulled his gun and waved it at the helicopter. Jercoff accidently discharged two .45 rounds, one of which took out an endangered Sand Hill crane migrating in a southerly direction nearby.

Blu watched the wounded bird plummet to earth, desperately flapping one vertical wing. Two rangers rushed over with sharpened sticks while another started a fire. It had been a long night. They were hungry.

We are all cavemen of a different time, Blu thought and started daydreaming. I wonder, he wondered, if I think hard enough, can I make diamonds out of dreams...no...but maybe charcoal, so I can burn em' again later. Blu lived for these moments of clarity.

≈≈≈

Yunger was slowly buried up to his neck by the fertile turtle. The rangers could have, but didn't, brush his face with a palm frond to keep him from suffocating on turtle moistened sand. They did, however, put flex-straws in his nostrils, like little snorkels. It was a kind gesture but didn't do much to ease Blu's discomfort. The problem was that there was one rule the rangers agreed with and therefore chose to obey, **Do Not Disturb the Nest.** Blu was part of the "nest." The rangers got Blu on that one and milked it for all it was worth. Every time Blu threatened to get up and leave, his mouth was filled with sand and although he smiled, it became more difficult to remain reasonable.

Blu daydreamed and fondly remembered the fate of

"Long John Silver" in the movie of the same name. In the film, Long John is buried up to his neck on the beach, as the revenge questing pirates wait for the tide to come in.

After twenty-two hours, "Long Blu Yunger" was barely visible to the camera or the clothing optional gawkers. The TV crews began to disband. Their opportunistic curiosity sapped rapidly when a turtle groupie named Shelly informed them, "**Hel-like-lo!** Like ... ahh ... it like takes like two like months for like the eggs to like, hatch like, Duh?" The youthful groupie shook her green hair and walked away, not surprised that the media, or anyone over sixteen, could be that, like, dumb. "That's news to me!" a Miami Cherub reporter chirped. With those words he justified his existence and, with a weak grab at a persistent wedgie, he too moved away.

The day grew long. The younger rangers fired off a bone and checked each other for athlete's foot. Most of the old ones nodded out, but a few held hands and oiled their weapons while the others went quietly blind as they stared at the sinking sun. Blu stewed, the turtle turtled.

The boned rangers were tired and talked quietly among themselves. The males made drawings of bird genitalia, with sticks, in the sand. The women dug holes in the beach with their toes and squatted to pee. It was, as Shelly the groupie put it, "Like, nature."

Toward evening, one of the rangers posted a large yellow, NO TRESPASSING sign behind Blu's head. The remaining rangers squatted, ass down, in the fetid sand. Soon, the evening sun approached the horizon and began her descent into the distant, wet blue, blanket.

Encircled by yellow police tape, Blu leaned back,

spread his knees and longed for the time when there was nothing to forget. He watched the western sky for the heralded Green Flash, the moment when the setting sun rays pierce the surface of the water and give hope to modern man and tourists alike.

Unfortunately, the rangers stood in front of Blu during these miracle moments at the magic hour and the only miracle Blu saw was wet sand, and pieces of dead sponge, falling from the ranger's olive drab butt cracks. He thought he saw Orion's Sock in the western sky. It just wasn't the same as Orion's belt. Blu was tired of Nature's dirty jokes.

Since he was not allowed a vote regarding his circumstance, Blu waited for the reptilian experience to pass. He wished he knew the Lamaze technique. Would he have to pay alimony? Would he learn how to swim and eat jelly fish? Dad? These and other pointless questions haunted Blu as he stared into the dark, sparkling void. Are stars just peep holes into the bright world beyond?

To keep his mind active, he said *doily* over and over until he lost count, at one-hundred-thirty-two, and fell asleep.

≈≈≈

The next morning mama turtle was gone, back to the generous sea. Eighty-two tiny turtle eggs were left behind. Blu was alone, except for a small cadre of rangers who slept in tents nearby. Last night's display of God's random nature reminded him that the greatest forces on earth have no shape. Wind, light, water, sound, fire, fear, smell, thirst, hunger and love. He'd experienced them all, all but one.

Later in the morning, after the remaining unhatched

turtle eggs had been gathered and "moved to higher ground," Blu noticed fires being built and frying pans emerge from knapsacks. He smelled Oleo and garlic! Several of the rangers noticed Blu's familial interest and grabbed large, smelly driftwood sticks. As a tribe they approached Blu...and goosed him from the nest. Ouch! The prodding was merciless and the rangers sent him on his way without even a howdy-do, a Park Service baseball cap or a certified Turtle Birther badge.

Blu felt soiled and used. He walked to a nearby car wash and followed a VW Beetle in. He was ashamed to let the swirling brushes beat him, but at least he was clean and enjoyed the blow-dry cycle, until the cops came. After a few succinct questions the officers took him to the Ranger Station where they discussed Blu's case over *Cafe con Leches*. Four rum-laden *con Leches* later, the Park Service agents agreed to pay for Blu to undergo professional rehabilitation.

However kind the gesture, it didn't help, because when Blu arrived at the Ranger Station's *Monetary Disbursement* desk the funds were, quote, "Not available at this time." Unquote. Blu was issued fifty dollars in food stamps and bussed to The Turtle Rescue Mission and Day Spa, in Key Larvae, for rehab. He was put in a ward with other turtles to be treated, counseled and prepared for eventual release back into the wild.

Turtle people sure are stuck in their ways, Blu thought on day one of his captivity.

During the admission process he talked to several stiff Turtologists regarding his emotional struggle. He talked about the pain of not knowing his offspring, the fruits of his loom. They may have been fried or, heaven forbid, scrambled. Those problems and his need for cash were discussed at length. The Turtologists got the cash part. The emotional aspect seemed to elude them. He didn't bother pleading. Blu knew some people would protect their ignorance to the death.

Blu was tired and walked the halls of the turtle hospital like an old cowboy. "That danged turtle changed me almost forever, sure, it's good to be famous, but two full days, buried ass first in wet sand with a hangover, was not what I had in mind," he grumped. A morose loggerhead, recuperating in a wheel barrow after a sex change operation, vented its agreement.

Blu was angry, angry at the world and at himself.

After two days in captivity and sick unto death of sitting in a glass tank with two emotionally disturbed Kemp-Ridleys, Blu borrowed a large Leatherback turtle shell from the display case. He lashed it on over his hospital smock, the one that wouldn't stay closed in the back. With a mouthful of lettuce left over from dinner, Blu put on his best turtle face and, with grim determination, crept through the reception area and out the front door on his hands and knees. The staff pretended not to notice. For some deep and unexplained reason he wanted to dig a hole in the pea rock parking lot, but knew he had to keep moving.

Blu pawned the turtle shell in town, bought some clothes and a ticket on the shuttle bus to the Keys, the new and independent *Gayhound Buzz Line*. The bus line consisted of an old school bus painted pink with black letters. The advertising brochure on the side proclaimed it to be the "Queen of the Fleet-We Can Go Fast, But We Can't Go Straight!" The Queen was idling in a ball of familiar-smelling smoke and almost ready to depart for Key West when Blu approached and had his ticket punched. The punched chad fluttered toward the ground and got stuck between Blu's flip-flop shod toes. Blu ignored the imagery and boarded the Gayhound.

The colorful vehicle headed down the Keys toward Key West where water was a popular molecule. Blu liked molecules. They have polar ends and Blu was into polar now. "... nor sticking to the edge of a beaker, myopic voyeurs preceded the flame, mooning sun's callous fingers, fumbling for God's faded nostrils, they had failed Cartucci, again ..." These words alone, spoken by a long dead, third grade science teacher were enough to encourage and comfort Blu, like lacing your fingers together, putting your elbows on your knees and your thumbs between your eyebrows.

Blu did just that on the way south. He had to turn sideways in his seat to accomplish it. The road was rough. They turned west. The road was still rough. It helped Blu focus.

Blu smelled French fries and fish foam in the air. He stuck his nose out an unsealed window crack. His nostrils inflated like a skydiver with a bad chute. A stink bug slammed into his front teeth and a no-see-um traveled up Blu's left nostril at 58 MPH. Three miles-per-hour over the posted speed limit, Blu noted. The unlucky *Ceratopogonidea* augured in two inches from Blu's brain and died in less than fertile ground. Blu snorted the bug out and onto the window.

The *Gayhound* gallantly pounded pavement across failing roads and broken bridges. Bald tires beat reggae rhythms on the snappy concrete cracks and, neglecting the deteriorating infrastructure; seagulls screeched like worn brakes and dive bombed for bugs in the shuttle's wake. Blu was headed south, back to his island in the fun.

Looner Too

During the same period of time that Blu was out of town, Ferling Bagwidth also left Key West and traveled by bus to Washington, DC in an attempt to market the Looner-Too. After three months of face to face, in-office consultations with his local Congressman and not showering or changing his cloths once, the government agent agreed to pay citizen Bagwidth two-thousand-one-hundred thirty-seven dollars and ninety-four cents for five fully combat-ready Looner-Toos. They also purchased ten shares of Loontec LLC preferred stock, to be issued soon.

Bagwidth struck the deal, took his advance payment, and caught a bus to Miami where he transferred to the new *Gayhound Buzz Line* headed for Key West.

The *Gayhound* approached the Last Gasp Bar in Homestead. The international road block was gone, but hundreds of coconuts, half smoked joints and sun-dried condoms lay scattered along the roadside.

Ferling squirmed and then rocked up on his left cheek, the victim of too many cheap hot wings. The bus made a hard right-hand turn. The timing was perfect. When the rubber tires squealed, just like the Looner-Too, Bagwidth fired on impact. There was some polite gagging. Windows were slammed open, emergency levers pulled, cheap cologne sprayed, Bics flicked but, after a few minutes, the passengers, not sure who to blame, settled down as they are wont to do.

Bagwidth was unfazed and had little concern for any danged decorum. Why should he? He'd made it big. He was on the *Gayhound* headed home, the Hero of Dung Beetle Lane.

"Got me a check for four hunnert and fifty bucks," he said under his breath and smiled. He fondled the wad, (we must assume it was the wad,) of cash in his pocket. And, like a drooling Labrador chasing a chewed red ball, the smoking *Gaybound* raced to fetch the spluttering sun.

Bagwidth didn't notice a small female passenger sitting next to him. Just moments before she had abruptly moved to another seat, then sometime later, moved back.

≈≈≈

The bus stopped in Big Spine Key. Blu awoke and took advantage of the stillness to make his move. Driven by necessity, he stood urgently and headed toward the air-conditioned lavatory in the back. Without warning he bumped into an old geezer who jumped in front of him.

"Watch out, you old geezer!" Blu sputtered.

"Hey, don't call me a geezer, you dick-brained frog fucker!" A familiar tone, an odd, yet familiar cadence struck a chord with Blu.

"Uncle Bag?"

"Shit!"

"No, it's me, Blu."

"I know it's you, you fucking idi–!"

The bus lurched forward throwing Blu and Bag toward the back in an insalubrious, velocity-induced and visibly awkward embrace.

The small passenger shook her head and watched

from the sidewalk as the bus pulled away. She would remain unknown.

≈≈≈

Blu and Bagwidth arrived in Key West. The *Gayhound* stopped and let everyone off at Dog beach. Bagwidth took a pink cab home to Dung Beetle Lane.

Blu walked downtown. He'd been thinking about a drink and needed a drink to think about what he should be thinking about.

"Thinking is a lot like fishing," Blu's mom used to say, "even if you don't catch nothin', it's still fishing."

≈≈≈

Perki Mellon, descendant of Sophie "Big Melons" Mellon, tended bar upstairs at the Naked Bunch on Duval Street. The Naked Bunch offered a clothing-optional rooftop saloon called the Neutrino Lounge. A hand painted sign above the stairway read, "We're all just passing through..." The Neutrino Lounge was a place where people who shouldn't, paraded around naked displaying their wrinkled members to a standard fare of nearsighted gawkers and uninterested ultraviolet rays. The Neutrino made as much money selling "Private Parts" sunburn remedies as it did selling drinks. Perki called it a "Members Only" club.

When Blu came through the door, Perki was in the process of extracting one of her two ample, three-dimensional, bosoms from a frosty martini shaker. The evidence on her left mammary allowed no room for skepticism or lack of belief in the power and strength of a woman. This one knew what she was doing. Knowledge is the fourth dimension, Blu thought, not knowing why, or what it meant.

Perki finished making her "special" drink and set it on the bar in front of a two hundred fifty-pound nude man who, according to the tattoo in his butt crack, was from Saskatchewan. It was hard to read. Saskatch watched closely and was impressed with Perki's talents. He reached for his wallet. It was an awkward moment for everyone. Perki's red-ringed, coldly erect nipple bespoke her dedication and indicated its (the nipple's) continued and heartfelt yearning for a generous gratuity. By the time Saskatch returned with Canadian dollars Perki's nipple looked like a little pink pencil eraser on the first day of school. Blu had supplemented his diet with pencil erasers in kindergarten. He and Perki had something in common already.

The Saskatchewanian dropped his money on the bar and moved away; the vinyl bar stool stuck to his ass and went trekking with him. Perki approached Blu, "Whatcha' having Bubba?"

Blu had a few food stamps left and waved them discreetly at Perki. She nodded.

"I'm having a great time and I'll have what he's having. "Blu forced his eyes to further separate in all fairness to her unbridled, wide yoke bosom. A wooden medallion hung around Perki's neck, "Drink don't Think" was carved in small Gothic letters.

"Comin' right up, slick." Perki smiled and set about the mixing.

"What's your special called?" Blu enquired.

"I call it a Tittini." Perki steeled herself for the final step.

After a half-a-dozen tumbles, Blu watched Perki remove her left breast from the martini shaker, for the second time in less than two minutes. She's tough and probably right-handed, Blu noted. Maybe I'll invent the Penitini. Pleased with his new idea, but not sure if he could pull it off on a regular basis; he grabbed his drink and moved out onto the floor where he did the old "When in Rome..." bit and dropped trou'.

On a nearby lounge chair an overweight female gawker gasped and grabbed for her husband whose sunscreen-slathered skin provided no useable traction. The gawkess plummeted face first into her mango daiquiri. The tiny but colorful umbrella traveled up her nose and partially inflated. She didn't seem to notice.

At the bar, Perki wrapped a warm bar rag around her now blue nipple and, with the other hand, focused on Blu through an upturned shot glass. With the magnification she was able to observe that Blu had a larger than average nut sack. Perki knew average.

"Whatcha got in there, cowboy, a Yoyo?"" she hollered across the floor with a wise ass grin.

"Hell no, sweet baby cakes, I got me a tri-freekin'-fecta, wanna see?"

Nearby, an aging rump ranger sat up too quickly and let out a muted yelp when he ensnared his tiny member that resembled a Key West pink shrimp, in the mildewed lounge chair straps. A crowd gathered around Blu. The typical questions ensued. Blu'd heard them all before.

"Where'd ya get it?" Perki piped.

"It came with the package." Blu responded, using one of his better lines. Meanwhile, the old pickle smoker freed himself in a most unsavory manner and tried to get into the conversation by using a laser pointer to highlight his keen observations. "They don't make em' like that anymore," he lisped crisply.

Blu said "lisped crisply" fourteen times.

The red dot never wavered.

Blu was back.

≈≈≈

While Blu regaled the gawkers with a tale of his love for Fakyah, ah... Beth, Perki ran to the drugstore and bought fifteen disposable cameras. She doubled the price and sold them to Blu's fans. Perki gives good business head, he thought.

Blu could be a walking gold mine in this town, she thought.

Blu eventually stood up. Perki smiled. "This dang ball works better than a dog for picking up women and it don't cost nearly as much to feed." He put his pants on. Perki split the profit from camera sales with Blu. He was fifty bucks richer and decided to spend it all with Perki.

Later that evening, Blu and Perki walked the flagrant streets of old town Key West. Near the intersection of White and Mandible Lane the famous tune, "Don't Cry for Me Sergeant Tina," sung with undersexed gusto by a male impersonator, echoed from an all female guesthouse pool.

Perki liked the song and loved pools. She made a plan. She always made plans. She wanted to be in control of her life, but in her case the plans weren't actually plans, only organized hopes.

Shortly, they were in said pool fondling weightless objects and singing along with an old Bitch Miller recording.

Perki floated on her back. She felt safe, as long as her neck didn't give out. Her smooth face was smartly moored between high floating breasts and again, if her neck didn't give out, she would never drown. Perki looked like a tiny, pink face on Mount Rushmore. Her left nipple, caught in a ripple, was cop car blue. This woman would not lack for attention. Blu said nipple-ripple more times than necessary.

"You know what it's like making a living with your tits?" Perki piped.

"I..."

"It ain't easy, Blu, look at this. "

Blu looked down, up and around. There are so many unfinished dreams, so many lives in disrepair ...

South of the Odor

It's me, Beth. I'm back. Blu used to call me Fakyah. It was cute and I miss him. He's probably got a new girlfriend by now.

Well, after I got caught up in the damned *Areola* hurricane, I went and got kidnapped by Pepto freaking dismal. It seems like I fell into an enormous Chinese finger trap. The harder I fought the tighter it got, 'til I was compressed, like air in a hose. The way things are going, I'll be spit out without a second chance at this whole *life* thing. That irks me. Stanks don't it?

Point your toes on the way down, my mama used to say. But after my time with that wild Blu Yunger, I got some wisdom on my own ass. I don't make the same mistake more than twice. But right now, who's counting, I'm in Mexico trying to get away from freaking Pepto.

Listen, before he kidnapped me, he fed me good and we spent a few weeks in a nice room that overlooked Key West harbor. I left a note for Blu, but I don't think he knows where I'm at, or that I'm kidnapped. Dang. I was hungry, that's why I did it, and Pepto offered to feed me and do laundry but, after twenty-nine days of room service, I got tired of weird shit and I was full. He made me dye my hair, all of it, blond and put scented bee's wax and a small paper umbrella in my belly button. He wore a tie even when he was bare-naked. Then, he ran out of rings. I told him I was leaving. He pleaded with me to stay and do the thing with the necktie. "Juz one more tiempo with de tie, por favor, and dee pulling on dee neck and, and dee..."

"No Way, Jose." I told him.

Therefore, after what turned out to be a "failed nooner," Pepto stuffed Beth and her purse into a Wharf House Motel laundry bag and dragged her out of the room. With the help of a one-legged bellman, Pepto flopped her into the trunk of the Camaro. Beth could see the car was red through a small hole in the bag. The color matched her lipstick! She pleaded with him to let her go.

"Fuck Ya!" Pepto replied loudly.

"My real name is Beth. Call me Beth, godammit!" she commanded from the bag. No response. She garfooned deeply and asked him to call her Beth for a second time. This time Pepto tried, "Buh ... Beh ... Beh ..." but Cubans can't say Beth. He gave up, slammed the lid, got in the car and drew a small pencil line, on an AAA road map, along the coast from Key West to Mexico.

The overly sensitive bellman thought the Pepto's remark had been directed at him and started to let air out of the Camero's tires. Beth heard the sensual hissing. She loved the bubbering joy compressed air could bring and longed for her own air pump someday.

"Conjo!" Pepto screamed. He slapped a clammy twenty into the bellman's waiting palm. The one-legged bellman bowed at the waist and tipped over.

The trunk was small and stale.

I should have strangled that fat sumbitch the last time he asked me to do him with the neck tie. I sure as shit shoulda, Beth thought as the trunk lid slammed shut. "Jus leetle beets more, just leetle beets more," the asshole used to croak. What's one more freakin' jerk on a double Windsor?

In the trunk, Beth repeated the question over and over until she fell asleep. She wished Blu was there. He'd know what to do.

When she awoke, she worked the spare tire valve stem through a small hole in the bag and let the air hiss out at comforting intervals. It kept her from going insane.

Being in the trunk may have made the ride seem longer than it was. During the trip she overheard Pepto talking to himself and learned he was being chased by "Bro." A Bro he apparently owed ten large. "That fuckin' spinner don't scare me," she heard him say for hours at a time. But Beth figured Pepto *was* scared, which accounted for the numerous air thinners set forth during the trip. Beth was scared, too, and, in a way, she was glad to be in the trunk. Still, she was afraid Pepto was going to sell her in Mexico to pay Bro.

≈≈≈

Pepto sporadically stopped for food and gas and got both, even when he only stopped for food. He loved the Taco Smell restaurant chain and planned his route accordingly. After eating, he went into the restroom, washed his armpits with a soaked roll of toilet paper and brushed his teeth with a comb.

Throughout the trip, the imprint of Bagwidth's pogo stick on the hood remained a grim reminder of the *Injusticia* perpetrated on Pepto. The undeserved dent gathered rain water and a peculiar microorganism formed. The mysterious growth led Pepto to wonder how the slime managed to stay alive in the divot, at sixty miles an hour. That question, combined with Fakyah's non-stop trunk lid kicking, helped keep him awake.

≈≈≈

At the third stop, somewhere in the Louisiana Bayou, Pepto opened the trunk and pulled out a glinting carpet knife. He looked around, then quickly stepped forward and cut a small hole in the laundry bag. He stuffed in a taco. He performed this act of kindness every ten hours or every other Taco Smell. He was human after all, he reminded himself, plus the girl wasn't much good dead.

Unfortunately, he cut the feed hole in the wrong place and Beth rode across three southern states with a wide variety of tacos stuffed in her butt crack.

Inside the bean-scented bag she planned her escape. It was pretty simple, get out of the bag and run like hell. Simple plans are the best she thought as the miles ticked by. She wanted her vibrator but was lying on her purse and couldn't reach it.

The car stopped at the US/Mexican border but no one checked the trunk. She tried kicking and screaming but the tacos made it rather uncomfortable and her voice sounded like she had laryngitis. Her fingertips were blue. She hadn't pee'd in three days. Or had she? Her mind was fuzzy.

Two hours after crossing the border, in the village of *Donde Esta,* the dusty Camaro scrunched to a stop and Pepto got out. Beth didn't know where they were but she'd had E-fucking-Nuff of the trunk routine. She was thirsty, dammit!

"That's IT!" she gargled. She squirmed around in the

bag and got her feet against the back seat. She tried to say, "This shit is starting to get on my nerves," but her voice was a faint and painful squeak. Maybe the exhaust fumes are getting to me, she thought. Beth kicked hard and the back seat popped forward. Her high heels pierced the laundry bag and got stuck in the seat cushion. She pushed with her hands and squeezed part way out, like being born ass first. Beth grunted and crushed the remaining taco shells with her posterior cleavage. The beans escaped, but Beth was stuck.

A small Mexican child naturally smelled the tacos and peered through the Camaro's window. Beth must have looked like some kind of alien space amigo with a dirty canvas body and black bean lips. The kid screamed. Within minutes a *POLICIA* came strolling up.

"Que paso?"

Innocent bystanders pointed at the car. The kid ran and buried his face in an attractive woman's bosom. His mother kept looking for him.

Senor Policia approached the car, gun drawn. He peeked in, *"Holy Sheets, dees one beeg taco,"* he stammered. He opened the door, grabbed Beth by the taco hole and pulled.

≈≈≈

"Hey!" Beth pouted after enduring some uncalled for assistance. She scrambled out of the bag and instantly squatted to pee. The *Policia* was standing too close. The cop looked at his shoes. Beth looked for Pepto in the crowd. She saw him; his face was as red as her lips were blue. He knew his cover was blown. He couldn't do *nada*, zip, squat nor the elegant, diddly.

While the *Policia* rinsed his shoes in a nearby fountain, Beth grabbed her purse, casually put on red lipstick and bolted up the street. She made it almost twenty-five feet before a sling back went on strike.

"Fucking shoe!" Her normal voice had returned.

The cop caught up to her, "You are to be making *malo* speakings to me?"

"Huh?"

"*Primero* you are making water on deez shoe, he pointed at his wet and squeaky shoes. *Eee, Segundo,* you are saying to me 'ah-Fuck You'?!"

"No, I said, 'fucking shoe.'"

"Ah *Madre a Dios*, now you are to be making me have a madness..."

"Screw it. "

"Jes ... you needing dee glue. You are right. I am to make a looking for eet."

≈≈≈

While the cop was busy with himself, Beth crabbed away on one sling back. The other swung from the middle finger of her right hand. She didn't want to stop to put it on. It was tough sledding. Her butt cheeks were juxtapositioned and remained focused. They stayed in the game and carried the ball forward. To take her mind off the discomfort, she remembered the dangling Pine Thang, the skeeters in her teeth and eating tadpoles with Blu, ick! The good old days.

The Small Café

The cafe smelled of coffee and piss, like all the others at this latitude. A dangling fly strip over the bar was full and buzzing. Business was good. Squads of corpulent attorney flies corkscrewed the smoky air, trying to eat each other while consoling the doomed.

Beth, a rumpled, now blond-haired woman in khaki shorts, slipped through the beaded door. She shook a small piece of taco shell out of her shorts and hiked up on a squeaky stool with her back to the bar. She pawed through her purse and pulled out a tube of Super Glue. The broken heel was quickly glued to the wounded sling back. Beth arched forward to re-install her shoe. She looked around the café and wondered where "here" was.

She noticed a man, a stranger, sitting alone at the bar. He was ugly in a rugged way. He's kind of ruggly, she thought. With the repaired shoe in place, Beth lit one of her signature loofa and hash oil bones and took a black-hole toke.

I want to be an adult, she thought during the inhalation, but every time I turn around I'm in a situation where being one doesn't help. She exhaled. Stoned insects quit buzzing and crashed into the adobe mud walls. The ceiling fan, missing one blade, was an epileptic's nightmare, but provided the only movement in the pungent nanosphere. Bleached blond hairs blew sideways.

Thick white smoke jetted from her adrenalin-dilated nostrils. Her stop sign lips seized the fragrant spliff with a firmness a man would enjoy.

Beth pulled one elbow back and leaned on the bar. She crossed her legs, plucked a piece of loofa from her lower lip and glanced to see if the stranger had noticed her. He had and continued to. She extended a toe toward the ceiling, seductively heel-flopping her weathered shoe. With broken finger nails she plucked the smoking butt from her chapped lips and blew a perfect "O".

The smoke ring matured grandly and haloed the toe of her dangling sling-back. "Grainy," the watching man mumbled. He wanted a better view of this woman. Staring at the fly strip was getting old. He stood quickly, moved toward a table. Suddenly he felt suddenly dizzy.

The strap slipped.

The shoe dropped.

Her nostrils flared.

Wind ate the smoke.

Am I having a heart attack, the man wondered, as a silent small-caliber bullet exited his forehead.

Beth bent to retrieve her shoe. The spent bullet missed her and landed in a dog food bowl near the door. Ting!

The watcher collapsed onto, then under, a table. He looked up her shorts with dead eyes. The smoke ring was his last earthly vision. It was enough.

Beth sat up, re-crossed her legs, uncrossed her eyes and took another drag. Unaware of the assassination attempt, she looked for the stranger but couldn't find him. Oh well...maybe he's in *El Bano,* she conjured. After a smoky moment she got up. Gotta keep moving, she reminded herself and exited the small café.

An indifferent waitress tossed a menu on the stranger's bloody table.

Beth touched her hair. The sweet scent of gunpowder followed her through the swishing door. It's easy to get bored even if you're beautiful, Beth thought. She wasn't beautiful, but what harm is there in a thought? Beth flipped her still smoking loofa onto the street where heavy dew damp stones embraced it with a satisfied hiss. She stepped on the butt and pivoted ninety degrees, left. Within a single long stride her peach-perfect ass caught up and stayed, high and tight. The two haughty halves of a perfect whole created a rhythm even the rocks, blessed with eternal hard-ons, could appreciate. Step by step she altered proximate reality. But Beth didn't notice; she was busy trying to escape down another dark street. She was tired, missed Blu and wanted to go home.

Earlier in Key West

With Perki's help, Blu got a job at the Naked Bunch. It only lasted a few days. He made a lot of money but, after making thirty-two of his unusually popular *Penitinis* in a row, he got frost bite on his mixer. No one offered to take his shift and when he learned workman's comp did not cover this type of injury, he quit. He liked Perki. He liked Beth more.

Blu left Key West in search of Fakyah, now Beth. She was gone and Blu missed her. More than he thought he would. They had a history and Blu was, if nothing else, a history buff.

With the help of a bartender, and a one-legged bellman he met while attending a cock fight in the 800 block of Duval Street, Blu learned Fakyah had been kidnapped by Pepto and was probably in Mexico. "Somewhere in Mexico, to be exact," the bellman divulged for a healthy tip. Blu picked up a Texaco road map and drew a skinny line along the coast from Key West to Mexico. He calculated the miles. Miles is only distance Blu figured and distance is only time. I got time, he said to himself. He could do it and he did.

Blu refused to be a slave to moderation, and stayed awake for six days straight. It took eight stolen cars, a riding lawn mower, six bicycles, a Great Dane, a motorized walker, ninety two espressos, a kayak and one skateboard to get across this great country. To raise cash he sold some of the stolen cars on the way, others he abandoned. He wished he'd learned to steal airplanes instead; the drive was getting old. The last car he boosted was white and Swedish made. "It was your basic two-door Vulva," Blu later admitted. Blu Yunger ditched the white Vulva near the Mexican border town of *Donde Esta*, a rural rut with a few haciendas, a fancy hotel, a popular mass grave and one restaurant, *La Misma Mierda Vieja*.

Blu landed ass first in Mexico and, ever hopeful, sat down for breakfast in *La Misma*. He stared at twenty-three roach holes chewed in the mildewed menu. The words *Español Solamente* were stenciled on the cover. Blu could only say a few words in Spanish and *Hay problema aqui?* (Is there a problem here?) were his favorites.

He didn't say *Hay problema aqui?* and instead hesitantly ordered breakfast with other Spanish words he thought he knew. He said the words loudly so the waitress would understand them. Five small brown customers, wearing horse blankets, sat silently nearby. Their calloused hands covered their mouths to avoid ingesting a fly, Blu assumed. Blu heard some thumping behind the restaurant. Forty-five minutes later a moldy tortilla, in the company of three fried geckos, sunny-side up, slid to a stop in front of Blu. "Heer eez you odor, Senor," the one-eyed waitress said. Blu smiled in Spanish.

Oh well, he thought, after all, the menu *is* written by hand and my Spanish isn't very good. He pinched the scalded green heads and reached for the salt. In his periphery, he saw pesos change hands between the silent Mexicans. Some kind of game? Be alert Blu, be alert.

The one-eyed waitress seemed strangely amused and pocketed a few pesos from the snuffling, teary-eyed hombres on the way to the kitchen. Too much hot sauce, Blu reckoned and created another smile. Blu's mom used to say, "You get as many smiles as you give, my little earthling." Blu figured he suddenly owed a lot of them since everyone around him seemed to be smiling.

The third world ain't shit compared to the fourth he thought, but didn't know why. He tapped a wet salt shaker on the table. It was going to be tough going.

I thought I said *huevos*, not *geckos*. "Dang lizards stank," Blu mumbled and scootched himself to an upwind position. He remembered the good old days, the dangling Pine Thang and eating fresh tads with Fakyah, ah Beth. He made up the eating tads part. He drew the line at geckos.

Blu snapped his Walther P-91K gut knife open and scraped wet salt over the headless geckos. He grabbed a lizard by the tail and poked it into his mouth with his finger then licked the blade. After a couple chews he swallowed, burped and gripped the knife between his teeth. Blu turned and double eyeballed the muffling Mexicans. If there was a game going on, Blu wanted in. Do Mexicans play Bingo? He talked to himself in English and finally realized *he* was the game. Shit. Real funny, hah, hah. Blu flipped an "under the table bird" at the snuffling amigos. He said snuffling nine times. It didn't help.

His order of *Café con Carne* arrived last. Blu looked down, looked up, looked down, looked up and smiled at the waitress. He realized he needed to learn *español* or, learn to smile a lot. He poured sweetened condensed milk over the floating meatball and grinned again at the one-eyed waitress. "Grassy-ass, Snort-rita. Eat and Live!" It was quiet. She was quiet. They were quiet.

A fly buzzed his plate and directed Blu's gaze toward a stained, hand-written notice, thumb-tacked to a post near the table. It read, *"Donde es La Gringa? Llama me (a pay phone number) I paying plenty big monies for deez one beetch rubio! El Gran Frijole."*

Now, Blu knew *Gringa*, in Spanish, meant, "One without a dick." He also knew that *Rubio*, meant blond, but the *Donde* threw him. Blu gagged a gecko down and gazed out a nearby window. Gran Frijole? Hum.

A blond *Gringa* stopped in front of the *La Misma's* grubby glass window. She stretched and yawned. Blu stopped chewing and thirteen eyes peered out through the window. They converged at a single fleshy pumpkin patch. She was long, and getting longer ... she... she sorta looked like Fakyah, ah Beth!

It got warmer. Blu felt lucky and moved to the door for a better view. Fusion leached from a lecherous vision. Could that be her? Red sling backs- Check, skinny legs- Check! Hot damn-Check! Blu stared at the *Gringa* and his love for Fakyah reignited, like too much charcoal starter in the barbie. He wondered if you could make electricity from desire and earnestly dry-humped a large, ceramic flower pot in an attempt to test his theory. What Blu lacked in couth he made up for with unrestrained intent and a few innovative and darkly provocative clay pot moves.

The *Gringa* glanced toward the door then paused to light her crude looking cigarette. She took a drag, turned her head and exhaled. The pungent smoke coned out, like the after-burner on a fighter jet. It was a familiar smell.

She French-inhaled and, of course, immediately surrendered to the pungent vapor.

Could it be her? Blu gawked. The Gringa didn't notice Blu's gawk. Blu has a pretty big gawk.

Still, Blu had time to think. He looked down and in doing so reduced the eyeball tally to eleven. Why do I count everything, he asked himself for the tenth time that day. It was an irksome quirk that he had been able to control, until recently.

"Shit!" the *Gringa* yelped and tried to escape the bite of an antagonistic Tsetse fly. The fly's face reminded her of Pepto as it buzzed into the dusty air. Her heels felt like rubber. The fly winked at her! The sidewalk was soft. Must be that dang Texas loofa... Hoo lordy! That's some good shit; she thought and started to get dizzy. She dropped, ass first, onto the rock paved sidewalk and quickly put her head between her knees. In that instant a hot, silent bullet missed Beth and exploded the mildewed underbelly of a forgotten Piñata strung across the street in front of *La Misma*. The laughing horse blankets chinned themselves on the window sill to see the squatting *Gringa*.

≈≈≈

Blu had suffered a near Beth experience, and someone said, "Shit!" again.

In the same minute, a one-man powered *Poopa Rapido* sanitary relief wagon careened down the street. The brightly colored vehicle catered to tourists who were in burning distress after sampling wonderfully organic and entirely indigenous local meals.

If you could produce within a block it only cost 20 centavos. For an extra 5 centavos, the driver would turn the cart into the wind and pedal slowly.

But now the cart blocked Blu's view. He looked again and the woman was gone.

Was the shot intended for Blu or Beth? Only the wounded Piñata knew and it wasn't talking. Its sticky bonbon guts spilled onto the stone street, the Piñata was bleeding out. Blu didn't hear the shot, only "Shit!" But, he saw the damage and knew what caused it and it wasn't a buzzard. He also noticed the relief cart had pedaled away quickly with a fat client onboard. The whole thing reeked of suspicious behavior.

Blu stood too quickly and had to sit back down; during which time he decided he loved Fakyah. She was like a Raman Noodle-hot, quick and cheap. It must be Fakyah, ah, Beth, he said to himself and stood slowly this time, ready for the hunt. Blu flipped some centavos on the bar. "*Grassy ass senor*, Blu said to the bartender's back. The barkeep nodded, "*Vaya con carne, amigo!*"

Blu headed out the door and tried to pick up the *Gringa's* tail. Trail.

Alone, and amongst unwary strangers, Blu Yunger felt oddly at home.

From the Fancy Hotel bar across the street, Blu overheard tinkling cocktail conversations that ebbed and flowed with the predictable cadence of canned laughter. He saw wrinkled, paper bag faces, painted pretty with eternal smiles, full of hope, civility, trust funds and cheap pharmaceuticals. The younger boozers sucked down the bootleg hooch left un-swallowed by the elders. Others, with lips far too thin for the tropics, chirped in clammy harmony. The joint was called *La Copa de Falso*

Horizonte, The Club of False Horizons.

≈≈≈

Blu stepped forward and joined the dark night in search of Beth. At the corner of *Calle Uno* and *Calle Dos,* things took a turn for the worse.

Blu made a hard left and walked into a hard right. He smelled hot sauce and bean dip with a hint of cilantro on the attacker's knuckles. Blu's face caved in like a deflated soccer ball. His clever thoughts and bony body hit the squelchy street at the same instant. Blu didn't have time for a *"Porque?"* or even a freekin' *"Que paso?" Nada.* Zip.

Blu was knocked out long enough to get rained on. The rain smelled funny.

He dreamt about his dog (although he never had one) and woke to find an alley mutt licking his face. He slowly regained consciousness. "I think I may have been sniffed by that dog," he mumbled vacantly. "First a fly, then a turtle and now a danged dog, what is it with me and animals?" Devoid of answers, Blu headed for a cold *cerveza,* a wet and nurturing beacon of hope and hops, in troubled times.

≈≈≈

Blu began the healing process and staggered into the nearest cantina a dive called *Dos Huevos.* He scratched his ass. His wallet was missing and so was Fakyah, ah Beth. Blu ordered a *cerveza,* which you can do anywhere in the country within a ten-foot radius. He got a line of credit with the barkeep by saying he was a convicted felon from the States. "Yeah, me too, it's one of the perks," the barkeep burped. Blu sucked down a cold one and gently probed his flattened nasal passages. He knew Fakyah, if it was Fakyah, was in danger. Her new, bleached blond hair threw him at first but now he liked it. She looked like a beach bunny in *Beach Blanket Bingo!*

It was still hot, still smelly and still Meh-hee-ko when Blu stuck six handmade toothpicks between his misaligned teeth. He locked his lips and blew hard. The effort inflated his crumpled face but, unfortunately, jettisoned one of the toothpicks across the room where it imbedded in a rotund waitress' ass. Her name tag read Consuelo. Consuelo got angry, but the customers loved it. Some of the single men offered a "cheek check" to look for damage.

Consuelo was rubbing her ass and crying when an old shaman stumbled through the dusty sun-shot door. He appraised the situation, "Snake bite!" He dropped his horse blanket, dove under Consuelo's skirt and started sucking the wound. "Must drive plenty bad spirits out of wound," he mumbled between sucks. It was native medicine at its best. Suddenly the old medicine man broke suction and yelled, "Boil water!" The old geezer was on a run, ordering tea at a time like this! Blu was impressed. Even with lips that looked like lobster bait, the shaman got a pretty good seal on Consuelo's butt. The waitress, who outweighed the shaman by two hundred pounds started to get upset but, somehow the gentle sounds of the sucking shaman seemed to calm her, to give her peace and everything soon returned to ...normal.

Blu bottle fed his emotions four shots of tequila, spit out most of the toothpicks, chewed four white pills he got from the bartender and got ready to make his move. He stood, burped, hoped his credit was good and headed for the street. A danged fly strip almost took him out near the door! Blu struggled vigorously to free himself. His knees, which would normally have lasted years, had gone bad from bocce ball. He flailed. They failed.

It was touch and go until Blu made the door. One step out he crouched and heard faint high-heel tickings. Tick...tick...tick. The ticking's echoed down a dark stoned street. Surreal and vaporous smoke wafted from the humid darkness and haunted the adobe walls of *El Camino de Luna*. Blu smelled the familiar after-burner vapor of Beth's hot loofa and hash oil blend. He was south of the odor, down Mexico way.

Flaps Up, Gear Up! The odds weren't good. Blu headed upwind. He'd kept some Tequila in his mouth to help with the pain and prevent his face from collapsing. Tequila does not compress. Twenty minutes later, he caught sight of the *Gringa* when she paused to steal a yellow and red *bufonda* from a street vendor. She was smooth and moved on quickly. Blu passed close to her body. It's her! He sneaked the purloined *bufonda* from her pocket and handed the scarf back to the old Mexican shopkeeper whose weathered, expressionless face, blind white eye, missing ears and red-stained toothless gums said it all.

Blu's mom used to say, "Love happens, but certain kinds of love happen quicker."

Blu followed Beth's red, piston-pumpings at a distance. He swallowed a little more booze and bayed quietly, like a great horned hound on the scent of wobbly-legged love. He knew Beth needed help and one thing the Yungers are noted for, Blu reminded himself, is helpfullnessedness.

When it came to love Blu had an untamed mind and a house-broken heart.

Should I let her know I'm here? After all, even though it was involuntary, she left me. Blu contemplated.

Beth kept moving and continued to worry about how to get home. The problem, she didn't know where home was. Finally, she decided what to do.

≈≈≈

Not far away, Pepto also decided what to do and looked for another ambush site from which to take a third shot. He was pissed at Fakyah, still couldn't pronounce Beth and was scared of Bro. A tri-freaking-fecta! He needed her. Even dead, her liver and sling backs were worth a few bucks.

At the same time Beth and Pepto decided what to do, Blu decided what to do, too. He swallowed the remaining Tequila and caught up with Beth on *Calle Uno*. "Fakyah ... ah ... Beff, it's me ... Blu!" He tried to kiss her but a forgotten toothpick made things worse.

"OUCH! Dang it! Your shirt's wet, it stanks and open your lips when you talk. Is that a worm on your tongue? Dang it, Blu, is that you?"

'Yeath, I think thso."

"You're not sure? What are you doing here? Where's the rest of your face?"

"I mithed you, and, well, I came to save your assth," he mumbled through clenched teeth. He was afraid his face would collapse if he opened his mouth too wide. Had his palate been compromised?

"From what?"

"Well, what about Pepto for sthtarters?"

"Oh, fuck him. He doesn't know where I am. I escaped!"

"You didn't notice the bullet?" A tattered toothpick slipped out between his lips.

"What bullet? Don't you get weird on me, Blu."

"Don't you get weird on me, neither."

"So why did you come here, really?"

"Well I, ah... I...it...ah, it *might* be love, too...I...? "He coughed to cover his words. Another toothpick slipped out.

"You *might* be lonely."

"Hey, I could be lonely back in Key Weird; I didn't have to come down here to do it."

"Oh yeah you did baby Blu... but, hey, that's the good thing about lonely, you can be it anywhere."

As much as Blu liked thinking about love, he was not prepared for this school of thought and instead of thinking, which took too much time and effort; he grabbed Beth and pulled her toward the imagined safety of the Fancy Hotel. A place where the "right sort" of people gathered, he hoped. They paused when they passed the assassinated Piñata in front of *La Misma*. The gutted paper carcass twisted in the wind. Blu told Beth about the gunshot.

"Oh, shit." Beth said.

Blu's tongue still felt funny, kind of gummy, when he said "Beth."

On the way to the Fancy Hotel, Blu pulled the last toothpick out of his mouth and sang an old rock and roll tune to Beth, "...Turn off the lights... don't try and save me, I just might be the lunatic you're looking for."

"Oh, Blu," she smiled and squinted her eyes.

The Fancy Hotel bar resembled a large fly strip and was swarming with ex-patriots. Their wrinkled elbows embraced the bar at diverse angles of despair and inappropriate comments filled the air like cheap cologne. Only one of the two dozen men and women appeared to be sober. Closer inspection might reveal the sober one was either asleep or dead. The couple entered the Fancy. Without warning, a red-faced, corpulent ex-pat stood on his chair and delivered a thunderous toast to a burnt out lighting fixture. "To all the things we don't know, and the grand fucking opinions we have about them!" The patrons laughed but their bodies didn't move; their wrinkles absorbed most of the motion. Still, their eyes twinkled and they guffawed deeply. Too white teeth flashed falsely in the smoky light.

Beauty is only skin deep, Blu thought, and there was some thin skin at this inn.

Beth swizzled towards the bar and Blu followed behind, using her butt for cover. He repeated "Beth's butt" eleven times. His still bleeding, deflated soccer-ball demeanor discouraged casual conversation.

Blu thought he heard his nose hairs whistling and, for some reason, contemplated the effect of Teeter-Totters on modern society. He had always been faked out on Totters and his coccyx still hurt.

Cautiously, Blu approached his current situation. It was a time and a place where a choice, or at least a distinction, between the precepts of conventional morality and a festering nodule of narcissistic inclination, was vital. Of course, Blu didn't know he was thinking this high level stuff, in those terms, but he was.

Blu heard a clock tick-tocking. Making, marking, and mocking the moments of his life. He made a decision but, watching Beth's long legs, quickly forgot it. Her sling backs chattered to hungry, hair-filled ears. Beth knew how to invoke another dimension and noticeably disturbed the proximate reality on her way to the bar. She was the ripple in the pond. Blu showed symptoms of low blood pressure and a premeditated buzz.

Things were coming together. It would be a good night.

≈≈≈

Germaine "Funny" Fundosa sat at the bar in the Fancy Hotel. He spotted Beth the minute she came through the door. A bad *hombre* with a messed up face followed her in.

Funny was a talent scout for the notorious *Fume Blanco-Mucho Mellow* cartel. He was always on the lookout for talent. For someone who didn't look like a crook, which was hard to find in ex-pat Mexico. He needed someone to work as a "drug mule" and tote weed across the border and into the States.

Until recently, The Fancy Hotel had been a good but tricky recruiting station. Many of the old rich folks, mostly women, were terminally bored and agreed to take any chance just to "Liven things up!" "Put a little lead in the pencil!" Funny knew ladies don't have pencils but he was not one to ruin a good line.

Funny was broke and desperate, but still, strapping twenty-two kilos of Sonora dirt weed on one of the eighty-year old ladies at the bar and sending her across the desert, with only a compass and personal lubricant, could be a gamble.

Only one of Funny's fabled *Gray Mules* had made it across during the last year, her name was Monique Satchel.

Monique was a Cherokee Indian vacationing in Mexico from Georgia. Unfortunately, on day three of their vacation, her husband, Running Nose, tragically discovered that he was not Pinto bean tolerant. During a complimentary lunch at Senor Pinto's Mexican Bean Brewery, Running Nose, who had never tried Bean Beer, died suddenly from an overly aggressive onset of Native American "Wind Spirit." The spirits talked. No one needed a translator.

Monique Satchel was tired of the "Real Cheap Pueblo Vacation Package" Running Nose had purchased and, now that he was dead, well, she was not emotionally inclined to stay around for the funeral.

Instead Monique gave the undertaker fifty dollars US, two of Running Nose's male enhancement pills, shook his hand and took a job with Funny. She would leave her past behind and become the romantic heroine, *Monique Satchel, Drug Mule!*

At the same time dirt was shoveled over Running Nose's papier-mâché coffin, Funny dropped Satchel's ass off near the Texas border.

Three months later she showed up in Ohio with chapped lips, a well-worn buzz, pregnant and only one ounce of dirt weed left.

Funny got screwed on that one. Still, over the years he learned to accept such vagaries and looked again at the doorway. The new girl gave him hope. "Hope eez like dee hard on," he mumbled and wished he hadn't. But today,

Funny was on the rise.

"Everybody is looking at me, Blu." Fakyah whispered.

"So am I... ah... I mean good, good. That means they're normal."

"What's that? "

"What's ...what? What? Never mind, look, let's get us a drink so I can think."

"About what?"

Blu stood silently and paused to reflect... I got all my sails up in the middle of a shit storm. Dang it, what have you gone and done to your ownself now, Blu Yunger? He scratched and let his dreams ferment. Can you make good wine from sour grapes, he wondered, without knowing why.

Funny Fundosa approached the bar. "*Buenos noches,*" Funny said through a wrinkled brown nose.

"No nachos, Grassy Ass," Blu responded. He thought Funny was a waiter.

Funny switched to English "I am the one known as Funny. What is beautiful woman name?" He stared at Beth's breasts.

"Fakyah," Blu replied for her. Funny continued ogling. Blu reacted and tried to say Beth's breasts as fast and as many times as he could to distract himself. His default word "hoof" would have worked better since "breasts" still made sense no matter how many times you said it/them.

He got to seven "Beth's breasts" before Funny got his ass up on his shoulders. Blu noticed the awkward posture and obvious misunderstanding. He quickly corrected. "Ah, oops, sorry *el* man, she's an A-rab, her other name is Beth."

"Oh, ah, buh ... Beh ... Beh ..." Funny tried, but like Pepto, his native tongue could not pronounce Beth.

"Howdy, I'm Blu."

Funny reached to kiss Beth's hand in the Latin manner. Instinctively, Blu moved in front of her and received what reminded him of a classic four-finger Kenpo Striking Asp punch to his solar plexus. It took the wind out of Blu. His face turned a peculiar shade of purple. He sucked air and wanted to puke.

" Oooh senor, I am sorry for you! Maybe making to have some dreenks for you eez good, no?"

"Si, mucho grassy ass," Blu gasped. Things were looking up.

The drinks arrived and, after several minutes of polite insults regarding the other's failing culture, Funny got down to business.

"You liking to make crime?" he queried.

"What kind of crime?" Beth asked.

"Kind for making plenty big monies."

"How big are the monies?"

"Oh! Many US dollars, green, in verrry nice bag, Gucci, bona fide Gucci! Only for walking in dirt."

"What kind of dirt?" Beth was on a roll.

Blu couldn't take it anymore but held his tongue. That, of course, made it difficult for him to speak. Beth continued, "Where is this dirt?"

"Eez only dirt, nice dirt in a line, from a point of A to a point of B. Eez not so far when you theenk how big the earth eez today."

"What's the earth got to do with it? And doing what in the dirt?"

"Oh, is only, how you say, just to make a carrying of, eh, ah, small leafs...eh...yes...green leafs... small, but many."

"How many small green leafs are we talking?"

"Each leaf only weighs leetle beets."

"How many little beets in all?"

"Twenty-two kilo of beets. I theenk."

Blu let go of his tongue and, although he believed we should talk to each other like we talk to our pets, exclaimed, "Hey, hold your buds, Dick-Weed! Are you saying what I think you are saying?"

"What you theenk I am saying?"

"What you just said!"

"Si?"

"You're asking me, if we, me an' her, want to risk our asses with armed men who fight the war for and or against illegal herb smoking? Huh? Is that it? Huh? Huh? Spit it out!"

"*Como?*"

"Perry?"

Beth butted in. "Look, Funny, let's talk money. I can git Blu to carry anything, anywhere, anytime. Right, Blu? Blu?"

"I..."

"Bluuuuu?"

"I..."

Funny interrupted. "Oh yes, dee monies. Today, only today, eez good day for you... ho, ho ho, so lucky gringos! Today we having beeg sale,"

"What kind of sale?" Beth perked up.

"For you, only today, we taking ten percentings from

any monies we paying to you, Funny is making a trueness for you to believe, my frien'."

Sounds good, and true, but is it too true to be good? They wondered.

Blu's mom used to say, "My dear little earthling, if something seems to be too good to be true...why, hell... try and git it anyway, occasionally some asshole fucks up and you win."

≈ ≈ ≈

According to Funny, success meant five thousand dollars US, minus "ten percentings," if they made it across the border. They were broke. It was a good deal and a chance they had to take. With one hundred fifty dollars in front money, Blu and Beth went into town, found an Army Navy store and spent it all. They outfitted for the long, desperate journey ahead. Blu bought jungle pants, desert boots and wart remover, a WWII Allied Victory condom along with acrylic calf socks, binoculars, fifteen canteens, a skateboard and a box of Q-Tips. Beth got a new organic loofa sponge, made in Texas, a signal mirror that could light a cigarette or fry ants and red zinc oxide for her lips. She flatly refused to make the crossing without her sling backs.

Now, Blu loved to watch Beth walk as much as anyone but high heels in the sand? Duh! He covertly tried to glue small Ping-Pong paddles to her heel spikes to keep from slowing them down in the fine granules, but she would have no part of it. Dangit. At the Goodwill, down the street, Beth bought some old coffee bean bags and fashioned a slinky desert dress with a slit up the front, back and sides. "I love ventilation!" she exclaimed.

Two days later they were ready to go. Blu's face was healed but he was still ugly. Funny met them at the Fancy Hotel where they loaded their gear into an old Morris Minor and headed for the border. The trash-compacted leafs were secreted in a large, dried cow bladder with custom goat intestine shoulder straps. It was cleverly painted to look like a Piñata.

After six hours the Minor coughed to a stop at a dry desert arroyo. Humble tumbleweeds tumbled across the unfruitful plain. Blu tried to hit the rolling weeds with a stone. A crude trail led off into the bleak tract. Blu unloaded their gear and, after fifteen attempts to skateboard in the sand, he kicked the useless board aside with a curse and looked for someone to blame. What will historians think when some archaeologist finds this skateboard in the desert a hundred years from now? Blu wondered. He knew the answer. So do you.

≈≈≈

After a few moments of embarrassing silence, Blu constructed a small travois using a blanket and two gnarly *mokobobo* bush sticks. He lashed the piñata named Herb, onto the frame and stared across the granular terrain. Beth's red sling backs provided the only counterpoint to the forever-reaching earth tones.

The desperate couple looked into each other's dry eyes. Blu folded two Q-tips in half and placed the frosty ends of each into both his and Beth's nostrils. It was an ancient method used to prevent inhaling too much dust, too much "desert dandruff," according to Funny. Fuck Funny! Blu and Beth hugged and, hand in hand, set out across the hot sand toward an unmarked border rendezvous. They had food and water for eight days. It would be the adventure of a lifetime.

Several steps into the journey Blu pulled out his binoculars and stared at Beth's ass. Then, between her knees he spotted a black station wagon, with the windows down, in a gulch less than a hundred yards away. A pungent scent wafted toward them and they heard Willie Nelson's "Whiskey River" blasting from warbling woofers. Blu looked back at Funny with a quizzical expression.

"Sí! Sí!" Funny yelled in encouragement, gesturing with the back of his hand, "Eez heeem! Eez heeem! ... Go! Go! Rapido! Eeez Beeg Monies, Beeeeg Monies!"

Blu and Beth dragged the bundle a few hundred feet and rendezvoused with the pick-up guy who grabbed the festive bladder and threw it into the station wagon. The rough-looking character reached behind his back and pulled out a wad of cash. He flicked through a few bills and palmed Blu eight hundred dollars. "Get the rest of your money from Funny the Fuckwad," the driver said with a toothy grin. "Is that a fucking Q-Tip in your nose?" The pick-up guy grinned and pulled away into a fast-setting sun.

The gringos were dusted with fine sparkling particles. Blu rotated and looked back. Funny was gone.

Beth jumped up on tiptoes ... "Blu, Blu, look at me, Blu! I look like Tinkerbelle!"

Blu pulled the folded Q tip out of his nose. "Fuck."

"Fuck."

Two faint "Fucks" faded in an unforgiving land. There are no echoes in the sand.

Beth plopped down hard on the rickety travois and

refused to move. Blu pulled the Q-Tip out of her nose and grabbed a piece of tofu jerky. He took a chaw then lifted the wooden poles and dragged Beth's ass towards the north. Her red shoes left two small furrows in the dirt. Good for planting beans, Blu caught himself thinking. He toiled on for forty-five minutes before spotting a truck stop with a gas pump, air pump and a diner.

When she spotted the air pump, Beth jumped off the travois and ran across Randy Cooter's Cowbone Truck Stop parking lot. She ran like a chicken escaped from its cage. Her sling backs threw diamond-dusted rooster tails high into the Halogen-bright desert air. Beth was a sight to behold and behold Blu did. Also taking part in the beholding was a trucker named Ticks.

Twelve Gears and Gone

Ticks Ratfield sat in an old White Freightliner tractor/trailer rig. He was fueling up at Randy Cooter's Cowbone Truck Stop near Del Rio, Texas on the Mexican border. Ticks one-hundred-twenty pound cowboy body shook in sympathy with the ancient diesel that rattled like an overloaded washing machine. I'd rather be riding a Brahma bull, he sometimes thought, and sometimes did. Ticks carried a load of squealing hogs in the trailer, bound for slaughter in Alamogordo.

Now, Ticks was a real cowboy and not one to cotton unto weakness but he, he, had a danged weakness of his own. He was a lonely dreamer. And now, in this moment of continued need, the Spirit of the Sand sent him a sign in the form of a blond-haired woman, running out of the desert wearing a pair of red sling back pumps. It was a dream he'd had since he started driving the big rigs. "I'll be hornswoggled! There she is, my all day daydream! And it looks like she's a-headin' straight fer the air pump."

Ticks rubbed his eyes and chin at the same time. His tanned leather face looked like a crumpled Tootsie Roll wrapper. In the same moment, he noticed a man in WW II army fatigues emerging from the bush. The man dragged two sticks through the dirt behind him. Nice furrow for beans, Ticks caught himself thinking. The stranger was following the blond woman. The man might be a stranger in these parts. But the woman, Ticks could tell, was no stranger to her parts.

Ticks sensed danger and did what any good man would do. He jacked the big White into gear, stomped on the gas and blew the air horn. HOOOONK! The passel of passive porkers suffered an unaccustomed G-force and hit the back wall en masse. Had the hogs been standing in a line, several tons of startled protein could have turned into an ungainly sausage that looked like a two-ton centipede with a wiggly pink tail.

Ticks plowed ahead, hoping to cut between the stranger and the fast moving, endangered, double breasted, red-heeled, road-running dreamsicle.

Ticks calculated his moves and then hit the air-brakes with both feet. The now seriously perplexed passel of porkers shot forward into the front wall of the trailer. Numerous instant and obscene noises occurred, the air brake pump popped a pressure valve and the trailer jack-knifed. Hiss........

When the dust settled, Blu was taking a whiz on one of Ticks steaming tires, Ticks was trying to get his seatbelt undone but his cowboy hat covered his eyes and Beth, well, she was cutting the end of yet another air hose. Life for her would remain uncomplicated, until the quarters ran out.

≈≈≈

The boys pooled their quarters then waited and watched, captured by the sight of Beth conquering her most pressing air pressure needs. Shortly, the three perplexed personalities gathered up and formal introductions took place.

"Howdy, I'm Blu," Blu said, zipping his fly.

"Howdy Blu, I'm knowed as Ticks." Ticks pushed his cowboy hat up off his ears with a sucking sound.

"Howdy Doody." Beth panted. She squeezed the last bit of air out of the hose and threw it to the ground like used lover.

"Tex?" Blu tried to get it right.

"Nope, it's Ticks. They call me Ticks. I may be small but I got me a bad bite. And plus, I git rained on last!"

"Ah, yeah, cool."

"You folks look pretty rough. Do you know where you are at?"

"Earth." Beth said with innocent conviction.

Ticks liked her style. "Close, my dusty darling, real close ... This is Texas. So go on, jump up in my rig, Missy, you too, Mister Blu. If its earth you folks are hankering for why I know how to get there from here. Giddy up!"

The oily stink of diesel and compressed pigs hung in the air. The continuum of life went unnoticed and the arid desert absorbed their souls like water. The stink stayed put.

≈≈≈

"Stanks, don't it? Gotta light?" Beth bumbled to start the conversation. She fired off a bone rolled with a tampon wrapper and herb pilfered from Herb. Then she curled up next to Blu. The bone was smoked and gone before the boys could get a toke in sideways. "What's the plan, baby Blu?" she mumbled from near his armpit.

Beth knew if she put a question into Blu's mind he

133

would run with it until the air ran out, just like her. He'd run until there was nowhere left to run. Then he'd bury the idea and dig it up later. Good boy, Blu. Beth knew well that the dogs of men's morbid curiosity soon tire and even the wild ones eventually return for food and simple love.

She liked that characteristic about Blu and scratched him behind the ears when Ticks wasn't looking. The stench in the cab wasn't half-bad once the truck got moving and the Sonora dirt weed proved to be pretty good shit. Beth tripped out early, crawled over the seat and into the dank sleeper-bunk behind Ticks and Blu.

Beth farted, nodded out and caught some zzzz's. Ticks and Blu rode side by side in silence, except for opening the vent windows at certain required times. The chugging diesel burned liquid fossils and white-line fever set in.

Ticks turned the radio on and popped a Tic Tac into his mouth without moving his lips.

To Blu, the Tex-Mex stations sounded like someone set fire to a chicken coop and was trying to beat it out with pots, pans and shrieks. Ticks kept an insistent Latin beat on the steering wheel with his gnarled thumbs.

After a while, Ticks took notice of Blu's missing ear. "What happened to your ear, partner?"

"Lost it in a apple bobbing contest at a 4H show. I was young."

"I cain't stop looking at that hole in the side of yer head, man! Dang thing makes me want to puke." Ticks let go of the wheel with both hands and faked a hurl out the window. "Whoo-eee! That is ugliness in the flesh!" Ticks kept staring at the side of Blu's head.

"Chill," Blu said and put his left hand up to his ear

hole. He tried to make his hand look like an ear so Ticks would keep his eyes on the road. His arm got tired.

≈≈≈

After an hour or so Blu made the mistake of saying he thought it was cool how Ticks shifted gears. The White had an old style, twelve-speed, manual transmission.

Throughout the night Ticks shifted through one set of six gears, then pulled a lever and switched to a second set of six gears, double-clutching every time. It was a lot of work. But now, every time Ticks shifted, he looked over to make sure Blu was watching. Every damn time he shifted, Blu had to watch him. They were in hill country. If Blu didn't look, Ticks didn't shift. He'd run the old mother diesel up until the RPM redlined and black smoke poured out of her stack. Ticks wanted Blu to see the muscles ball up in his arm, muscles the size of a chicken leg.

Yeah, it's weird, but do-able, Blu thought, and inhaled the night wind. He caught a whiff of Beth's hair. It calmed him.

The driver's seat was badly worn so Ticks installed two lounge-chair cushions on top to prevent his "ownself" from dropping ass-first into the hungry springs. He sat about six inches up off the main seat, high enough he could see over the dash. His legs were short. He compensated for his lack of vertical accomplishment with a pair of custom, high-heeled, cowboy boots. Ticks could clutch, brake and throttle with his heels.

Blu also noticed that Ticks constantly let go of the steering wheel and used both hands to push his oversized cowboy hat up off his ears. Ticks mentioned earlier that his ears always hurt.

135

Blu dismissed the idea of suggesting a babushka and finally posed a reasonable question, "Well hell, Ticks, why don't you get a smaller hat?"

Ticks looked puzzled and focused intently on the voltmeter.

Blu reached behind his seat and pushed Beth's tongue in, then, having nothing better to do, he contemplated the hat situation. He soon spotted a pair of yellowed jockey shorts sticking out of the glove box. He got Ticks to put them on his head, underneath the hat, to keep it from slipping down and affecting his ability to see the road. Ticks' waist size and hat size were about the same. Blu steered the rig while Ticks donned the underwear, the jockey shorts looked like a nasty French beret flapping traditional surrender in the dry desert wind.

Ticks looked in the rear view mirror and adjusted his cowboy hat. He looked over at Blu and smiled. "You one smart sumbitch, Blu!" The faded yellow label was visible above Ticks' sunglasses. He looked like an underwear commercial gone bad, but Ticks grinned and leaned over the steering wheel and stared down the white line like a near-sighted sniper.

The pair began to talk and soon found they both liked Kenny Rogers and neither of them knew, as Kenny had suggested, "When to hold'em or when to fold' em."

"What do you do, Blu?"

"I'm trying to be a hero."

"How long you been trying?"

"Hell, I don't know, it comes and goes."

"Yeah, I know what you mean. You gotta be slicker than snot on a door knob to git by nowadays, know what I mean?"

"You betcha, Red Rider."

It was quiet for awhile. A while made of miles.

Just before dawn, Ticks pulled into a large, dirt paved truck stop, "Let's get us some grub."

Beth was still asleep. Blu and Ticks got out, locked the doors and moseyed into Wyatt Burp's diner.

Walking in his custom boots was difficult for Ticks and gave him an unusual gait. Blu couldn't help but think that Ticks looked a little like Beth, from behind. But, of course, everything looked like Beth from behind to Blu.

Beth. The word slid off his tongue and landed softly, like ice cream from a cone, like mud on a puddle, like sun on sand, like...shut up!

They entered the diner. With a cowboy flourish, Ticks took off his ten-gallon hat and started chatting-up the waitress. Her nametag read "Rosa." She was a nice-looking Mexican woman with long black hair, a big butt and a gold tooth in the front of her mouth. Rosa started laughing the minute Ticks took his hat off, but Ticks misunderstood and winked at Blu. Ticks prided himself on being a "swordsman" and had shared some of his graphic exploits with Blu during the trip. He'd told Blu, "Some women is just drawed to me, they surely is."

Ticks nodded at Rosa, "Man, she seems friendly, eh?" The words slipped out the side of his mouth. Rosa picked the Jockey shorts off Ticks' head with a fork and set them on top of his hat. Ticks' face turned red as a Texas sunrise and he gave an "aw-shucks" kick at the floor. He almost tipped over. Rosa caught him and laughed again.

They sat down. Ticks looked at Blu, looked in the area

of Rosa's nametag and ordered. "Rosa darlin', gimme some scrambled narrow face eggs and some rattlesnake bacon, hold the fangs!"

"I'll have the same." Blu piped.

Ticks laughed and got excitable. Rosa was already laughing and excitable. Blu was hungry. A few minutes later, the chicken eggs, Ticks called them "narrow face" or "profile birds," arrived and were consumed with gusto by both parties. Ticks farted, Blu burped and Rosa laughed. It was a good night.

They were about to head out when three dusty Mexicans walked through the door and started after Ticks. "Hey Gringo, that's my girlfrien'. What are you doing talking to her? *Porque* asshole?" one of the Mexicans chirped.

Ticks changed from lover boy to a ball of rock-hard meanness in a nanosecond. "I ain't doing nothing. I'm eatin' some danged narrow face. She's the waitress. Buzz Off! Compren-fucking-do?"

The Mexicans started to get abusive. It wasn't looking good. Is this the "It" that will change my life, Blu wondered and grabbed a few ketchup packets. Finally, the owner came out of the kitchen gripping a baseball bat. He was a right-hander.

"Get the fuck out of here, all of you," he said to the Mexicans in English. He looked over at Ticks and Blu, "Sorry about them jerks, guys."

"Hey, no *problemo*, we all got a little asshole in us," Blu responded and winked. Not sure how to reply, the owner faked a bunt to Rosa's butt and returned to the kitchen.

Ticks went into the bathroom, adjusted his hat and went outside. Blu was running around trying to take a whiz on tumbleweed. "Blu, git over here!" Ticks called.

They walked toward the truck parked near some dusty scrub pine. Some kids had toilet papered the bushes nearby. Suddenly, out of the weeds, came the Three Amigos. Striped with pink 3-ply toilet paper, they headed straight for Blu and Ticks. Blu tried the only phrase he knew in Spanish *"Hay probelma aqui?"* The lead punk didn't pause to answer. He walked forward with jerky rooster steps.

"See, Blu, they got their asses on their shoulders. It's bad for balance." Ticks watched them turkey trot towards the White. "You take the two on the outside, Blu. I'll take the guy with the knife."

"Knife?"

With bowed legs, high-heeled cowboy boots and a Stetson hat with undershorts sticking out the side, Ticks looked silly but did not blink or retreat. He conjured up some cowboy cool.

Blu pulled his belt off and wrapped it around his left hand. He'd seen it done in a movie.

The Mexican with the knife approached and prepared to listen to the skinny gringo beg for his life. Ticks talked softly with an innocent grin. El Knifo leaned forward to better hear the gringo's plea for mercy. It was the part of being a punk the punk liked best. The punk wanted to get this takedown on film, to show his fellow gang members and girlfriends. He reached into his pants pocket with his left hand for a disposable camera.

"Let go of that thing," Ticks said, pointing towards the

aggressor's crotch, "it'll grow!" Ticks winked at Knifo's buddies. "Neenee, nawnee, nooney..." he continued. El Knifo couldn't stop listening to the high-heeled trucker and looked down, toward his ridiculed chilli pepper. He did not notice that Ticks had him off balance. Mistake *numero uno.*

Ticks eased up in front of El Knifo, who was three inches taller. He winked again to distract the two evil-looking second-string punks then - ZOT! Ticks reached in toward the Mexican's belly button. "Coochee Coochee," he tickled with a whisper. El Knifo looked down again. Mistake *numero dos.*

Ticks instantly stepped forward, head butted Knifo's chin, slapped his arms apart, grabbed his head, held the hombre's knife arm back with his elbow and locked his hands behind the uncomprehending dusty brown neck. Using the Mex's head for leverage he jumped up, wrapped his legs around the Mex's waist and pulled his head toward him. After riding the staggering antagonist for a few feet, Ticks bit the Mexican's nose off. Blu could hear the crunch. Like the sound of a snapped bean! He had not seen that one in a movie.

It happened in less time than it takes to tell.

Ticks spit the brown nose out underneath his armpit. PHOOWEE! The pulsing snout skittered through the dirt. Ticks jumped off.

El Knifo freaked, dropped the blade and watched blood blowing out of the hole where his nose had lived. His eyes were crossed. "Holy Sheets!" he exclaimed and dropped to his knees to pray or, maybe to find his missing nose in the oily loam.

The right-side punk recognized the "snapped bean" sound and puked. The left-side punk screamed and ran back into the TP'd bush. "That stubby fucker won't be hard to track," Ticks noted wryly.

"Stubby Fucker, isn't he a musician?" Blu didn't wait for a response. He dropped his belt in the sand and checked his trousers for stains.

Ticks turned and looked at Blu, "You know, Blu that always leaves me a bad taste on my West Texas tonsils. Let's go have us another coffee."

≈≈≈

The pair walked back into Wyatt Burp's. Beth was still asleep in the tractor. Ticks started talking to Rosa again. He even told Rosa that he just bit her boyfriend's nose off. "Talk about blood, man! Holy Hay-Zeus!" He slapped the counter. Bottles of Habanera sauce tinkled politely. "They's some big fucking vessels in your nose, you know."

"Si." Rosa laughed.

Ticks had a glob of blood in his armpit where the nose passed by. "Dang Beaner winged me." He laughed like an idiot and tried to clean it off with a napkin. Rosa thought it was funny and poured salt on his shirt. They were both laughing like idiots. Ticks winked at Rosa, "Fucking Mexicans, I'd sure hate to eat a whole one ... wheweeee!" Rosa laughed again. Ticks was on a roll, "Leaves me a baaad taste." Ticks scrunched up his face and stuck his Texas tongue out. Rosa laughed from her soft belly. She must have seen a lot of crazy things in her day and found the best response was laughter. Plus she liked Ticks' style. Blu ordered an omelette, ate half of it and wrapped the rest in a napkin.

Blu tossed five bucks on the counter. Ticks patted Rosa on the ass and they headed for the door.

Back in the truck, Beth was still sleeping soundly. Blu pushed her tongue in, tucked a piece of the omelette under her nose and fastened his seat belt. The first thing Ticks did was look over to make sure Blu was watching. His chicken muscles were balled up high and tight. Ticks was ready for action.

The big White Freightliner coughed to life and they drove out of the parking lot. Blu saw the nose-less Mexican out his side window. The unsuccessful *Pancho Villa* had a rag on his face. He was still looking for his nose in the dirt. It would probably be even harder to find after Ticks drove over it on the way out.

"*Hay problema aqui?*" Blu hooted his one phrase out the window, then turned and grinned at Ticks. Ticks nodded approval and their private ritual began. Ticks hit the clutch, Blu watched. Ticks shifted into low gear. Blu watched.

An hour or so down the road Blu's adrenalin wore off. Beth twitched awake, ate the entire leftover omelette in one bite and stretched. Both men stopped breathing. Blu inhaled her scent and felt a stirring in his loins. His dry nasal passages whistled like a hungry young bird. Loins?

"You know, Ticks, we're not going a lot farther than here, so the next town is good for now."

"You got it, Red Rider."

Ticks would miss the girl, his wild-ass desert angel, his dusty darling, but at least his dream came true, once.

Half an hour later Ticks pulled off the road, screeched to stop and tipped his hat toward Beth. "*Vaya con carne,* my dusty darling." Before either Blu or Beth could say anything, Ticks nodded with a wink and slammed the Old White in gear. The ever-cheerful pigs, still bound for slaughter, oinked their last goodbye. The pair stood in the dust and listened to the sad squeals fade. Twelve gears, and gone.

≈≈≈

Blu started to tell Beth what happened.

"That guy, Ticks, well he, he bit the nose offa ..."

"Don't get weird on me, Blu."

"Don't you get weird on me, neither."

"Shit."

They looked around the deserted intersection.

"Now what? Are we screwed, Blu, or what?"

"Well, in order to be screwed, we'd, ah, have to, ah, screw." Blu turned slowly with, "that look" in his eyes.

"Oh, Blu!" Beth smiled and dropped her coffee sack dress in the sand. She was breathing hard. She knew she was easy, but, under the right circumstances, who isn't? It was her balancing thought.

"Run from me baby; let me catch you in the wild! Like salmon!"

"Ooh Blu... OK!" Beth giggled. Her naked body kept the promise her dress made. Her sling backs threw diamond dust against a desert sky. She hauled ass into the bush. She didn't try too hard. Blu cut to the chase and harpooned her in the sparkling sand. Call me *Fishmeal*.

During the melding, Beth noticed Blu's third orb and was about to make a wise-ass remark when she heard the rattlesnake. "Don't move," Blu said, then suddenly, and without warning, Blu orgated with a passion he had never known. His primordial grunting and humping intimidated the deadly snake who quickly surrendered to the much smaller, but obviously hungrier challenger. The cowed rattlesnake slithered away, dragging its flaccid rattle through the sand. Nice furrow for beans, Blu caught himself thinking. They made love under a sun burnt sign that read, "Pinhole, Texas -Pop. 8E2.

Finally, the hard breathers bumped to a stop and fell apart. They lay alone together with pounding hearts, fuzzy dreams and fresh coyote dung. In the after-glow of hot sand sex, Blu said Beth nine times to sooth himself. It was the first time she'd let him do it. Of course, it was the first time he'd tried. Beth sliced across the hot sand toward Blu and looked up with sweet puffy lips, "Oh, and thanks for the omelette, Blu man."

They eventually got up. Beth walked back and picked up her dress, put it on and adjusted her sling backs. Blu zipped up, but forgot his third orb and suffered a major groin snag on the upstroke.

He went down on his knees in the persistently hot granules. Beth turned to see him grasping his groin and moaning.

"Not again Blu, not now." she said, not totally serious. Beth breathed deeply and, like moths to the flame or darts to the board, they were drawn to Pinhole and the next chapter in the dog-eared chronicle of their lives.

Pinhole, Texas

The recently coupled couple arrived in Pinhole on feet. The only entrance not locked, blocked or cocked was the front door of the local church, The Holy Order of the Shrivelled Penance. The temple was a small adobe hut with a red Mediterranean-style roof and a crude cross made of dismembered, plastic pink flamingo parts. Blu peeked through the beaded door. A dark-robed sister blew candles on the altar. Brittle pieces of tile, mud and the occasional depleted pistol round dropped from the ceiling at odd intervals. Nearby, between the pews, another dark robe picked up spent .45 cartridges and used condoms, all apparently the remnants of the last service.

A tottering nun, wearing a boa made of hummingbird feathers and sporting six-inch heels, approached. "May I be making of helpings to you? My name is Sister Bruce, the Elder." The sister's lack of tits and deep voice puzzled Blu.

"Fruit of the Loom," Beth muttered softly.

"Pickle smoker," Blu bleeped in affirmation.

Beth took the lead, "… Ah Sis, this here's Blu, the Yunger, and I'm Beth the ah …"

"Beth." Sister Bruce repeated her name over and over with a lisp. He couldn't stop; he kept saying "Beth, Beth, Beth, Beth, Beth …"

"HEY, SNAP OUT OF IT, DICKWEED!" Beth

squawked with a piercing fierceness. Then, with a contrite smile, she looked the now-focused Elder in the eye. "Ah, look Sis, we're screwed and need some help."

"Screwed?" Sis snapped out of it. "Oh ... Si ... Oh my! Yes! But, here in deez place of many holies, it is only when the little big finger, on the clock, makes to pass the *cinco hora* that eet is time to do the, ah ... deed. You need place to, ah ..."

"Grassy-ass sister, mighty obliged." Blu chimed.

Sister Bruce quickly cleared a few crosses and whips and made space for the couple near the altar. It looked remarkably like anyone of a thousand Florida Keys Tiki bars. Things were looking up. Sister Bruce held her hand out and rubbed her thumb and index finger together. It was the old sticky booger move. "So much for the blessing," Blu mumbled and palmed Sister Bruce a crisp, green, twenty. Money green was the most beautiful color he had ever seen. It was the color of Beth's eyes when she looked at lettuce. Sister Bruce gave him a pamphlet describing the church's history, holy mission, sewage plan and a membership application to join the Holy Order of the Shrivelled Penance. He also got a free communion drink card.

It was an interesting scene, but Blu was tired and didn't bother to read the pamphlet or get the drink. His mind raced, but he forgot to put it in gear. Thankfully, Beth poked him with her soft finger and he moved toward the altar. He could still feel her eager body against his.

During the night Blu dreamed of hairy chicken legs. Beth dreamed of snakes. After a few hours sleep, Blu awoke and knew it was time to move on.

Check out time came earlier than expected.

Two centuries earlier, The Holy Order of the Shrivelled Penance had been allotted four *"especial"* sheep by the reigning diocese. And, lo, those sheep begat other sheep and the current flock of begattees were trained to perform holy yoga every morning near the sacred altar. Blu and Beth were in their hallowed space.

The flock milled nervously about. Blu stood too quickly and passed a sacred wind. The sheep bolted for the door and baa'd for mercy. Blu and Beth watched Sister Bruce tackle one of the escaping flockers by the ankles. With heavenly devotion Sister Bruce held on and was dragged into the street.

Beth fanned the air, "Yoga, again?"

"Not really." Blu finished a gulp of wine from a gold-plated goblet near the pulpit/wet bar. It was good, dry dirt, Cabernot with a hint of dust and donkey dung, Blu noted. He grabbed a couple of skinny white crackers and a monogrammed napkin for Beth. "Damn considerate if you ask me," Blu cracked, "Better than the typical Holyday Inn."

Beth sighed and popped a wafer.

They headed for the door with dry wafers stuck to the roofs of their mouths. Blu tried to say hoof "oof, oof," but failed. Beth wanted water, but couldn't speak. They were surrounded by low humidity. Her tongue, tired from trying to get the wafer unstuck, began to slip out. Blu was fighting his own battle with a wafer as a faint bell echoed through the holy chamber and a different sister appeared. "Hello chosen ones, I am Sister Todd, a Being of Light." Sister Todd twisted her moustache and approached with a clergy-like slink. She spun around and bowed, facing away from them. "Quaint," Blu thaid thoftly to Beth, "must be what they believe in."

"No thhit," Beth tongued in turn.

Sister Todd executed a perfect one-eighty in her desperately tight spandex garb with the familiar "zephyr window" in the rear. It looked like a bad habit to get into. Sister Todd straightened and wished them good luck, but instead of waving goodbye, she launched a well-manicured hand toward Blu, palm up. Blu noted the platinum Rolex on her thick wrist. "Musth be palm Sunday." Beth rolled her eyes. Another green one passed into oblivion. Blu got a free condom from Sister Todd but could not bring himself to envision what the "sisters" would do with his money. But he did.

The wafers wouldn't give up; they needed water. Blu took Beth's hand and stepped into the town square. Ringworm Circle, Pinhole, Texas - Pop. 8E4. They headed for a community water trough, head-butted a couple horses aside and stuck their faces in tepid, horse-slobbered, water.

Fork Q

Granny "Floy" Fracas lived on the Fork-Q ranch out east of Pinhole near the end of Old Boheel Road. Granny was eighty-two and had spent her entire life on the Fork-Q. She inherited the spread when her dad died.

Granny remembered a hard life, full of hard hardships and harder hard hardships. When she was young her dad made her walk to school. There was no school.

By the time Granny was twelve, the family owned forty acres of arugula, two chickens, a worm farm and one cow. Then, in 1952, grey wolves were seen in the area. Her dad, old Jumpin' Bob Fracas, set ten ACME animal traps around the pasture to save their cow. The cow got caught in trap #2 and the wolves, even the old gimpy ones with no teeth sauntered over and gummed on Bessy. Jumpin' Bob was pissed and, even worse for the wolves, Jumpin' Bob was a crack shot with a .306.

Granny always told folks how the family ate wolf meat for the next six months. "Why, me an' daddy Bob got a lot more meat offa them gamey wolves than we could've from that skinny-ass cow." It was one of her favorite stories and the one she told Blu and Beth when they arrived at the Fork Q, looking for a place to stay while they figured out what to do.

Granny liked the couple and informed them that staying on the farm entailed some work, work that included milking cows.

"You ever milked a cow, son?" Granny asked.

"Yes ma'am, I milked on one of them tits once when I was at a 4H show. It's where I lost my ear."

"Oh, you poor thing, let me see."

Blu leaned forward. Granny grabbed his remaining ear and took him to the floor without getting off of her rocker. It was over before it started.

"You fuck up at Granny's, you go down. Read me punk?"

"Yes ma'am" Blu tweaked from the dank carpet.

"All right then, Blu, you need to get up at four a.m. and go out and milk them cows. Then we'll talk about money."

"Yes ma'am."

Granny put them up in the barn and gave Beth an alarm clock and a breath mint. The barn was dark and smelly. The high-pitched noise of fast predators echoed in the dark rafters.

The alarm clock went off at four a.m. Blu got up, brushed some hay off Beth's tongue, pushed it in, and went to find the milking machine. There were no lights. He worked by feel. It was hard work. It was the Yunger way. Granny said she had six cows. Finally Blu got the rig hooked up. Only five more to go, he thought and flipped the switch. A moaning, like neither he nor anyone else had ever heard, rumbled from the barn. Blu ran outside. A great beastly roar echoed from within, then silence. There was no smoke or vibration.

Granny showed up in her flannel nighty, carrying a 12-gauge shotgun. Beth showed up in her underwear with sling backs on. The trio moved closer and looked inside the barn. They saw a large animal. It was not breathing. "Oh no! That's Lloyd, my prize fucking bull! Oh no!" Granny screamed. The bull was laid out flat on his back, all four legs in the air. With his head upside down, it looked like he was smiling, his lips were in the dirt. The milking machine sucked uselessly nearby.

"The milking cows are in the back barn, you freaking dip stick! You're outta here!" Granny roared and fired a warning blast into the air that blew the rooster wind vane off the porch.

≈≈≈

It was morning. No place to go.

At the edge of town they flipped a coin, spent twenty minutes trying to find it in the dirt and then started walking eastward along the nearby railroad tracks. Beth's sling backs made for slow going. After an hour, with the town still in sight, they came across a herd of bony range cattle munching near and on the tracks. The space between the rails held the greenest grass. Blu knew why.

Toot! Toot! Blu and Beth turned to see an ancient locomotive approaching from the west. It was heading for the herd. Ten odd-looking boxcars trailed behind.

Steel wheels squealed and pistons pissed as the old rig lurched to a stop twenty feet from the munching bovines. The famous, low pressure East Coast Raspberry Steam Whistle, bleated wetly for the hundredth time. The cows moved away slowly, but the rude whistle set off a chorus of screeching and hooting inside the fourth car back. Blu looked, "The fourth car is full of monkeys!"

"Stanks, don't it?" Beth chimed. A hand-painted sign on the side of the boxcar read "Big Mama Dingling's Fat

151

Ass Circus."

They looked at each other and simultaneously blurted, "It's our way out!" Blu said "blurted" nine times; he liked the word's action, then grabbed Beth's hand and headed for the caboose. The train began to pick up speed. Blu could see Beth was not going to make it. Damn sling backs! He picked her up and ran toward an open door. With a tremendous heave Blu tossed Beth into the ninth car. He made one last effort to save himself but ran into an iron signal post.

He grasped, gasped and looked up from the painful cinders. The last he saw of Beth, she was being pulled gently into a silverback gorilla's cage. The silver back eyed a sling back.

"Fakyah!" Blu screamed at the train's smoky ass. His girl was gone.

Face down in the dirt, Blu remembered the buzzards, old One and Two. He knew it was time to grow up. "Think I'll take a rain check on that idea," Blu said quickly to counter the heinous reflection. Suddenly, alone and confused, Blu struggled upright and, after testing the wind, headed east on foot. He reached into his front pocket and patted the remaining wad; we must assume it was the wad, of cash. A small smile escaped his dry Yunger lips.

Trout's Tale

Nothing counts ... unless you're counting.

It was time for Trout Bender to leave the small Florida farming town of Pooheepka. Pop. 627.

Trout walked slowly toward town where he hoped to catch a bus to somewhere. Anywhere would be somewhere compared to Pooheepka. He ambled along and thought back over the last few years.

Three years earlier, Trout arrived in Pooheepka after a stint with the French Foreign Legion. During his tour with the Legion, Trout traveled extensively and formally surrendered in many different and colorful locales around the world but, eventually, he just wanted to go home. Home to Florida and back to his tribe, the Turaquoi Indians. The Turaquoi, an offshoot of the Wannabe Clan, were an opulent and well-appointed group of retirees living in air-conditioned Tiki huts among the saw palmettos, scrub pine and run-off pits surrounding central Florida's biggest malls. Many of the early Turaquoi had been rounded up and put in mental institutions for trying to, "Save the Earth."

Trout's first job in Pooheepka was wrangling worms for a guy named Danny Quatrell who ran the Low IQ worm ranch six miles out of town. That job ended suddenly and now, a year later, his last job, circumcising snapping turtles for the county animal welfare clinic, also came to an end.

Trout ambled down the dirt road in a cloud of warm, insect-laden memories. He carried his belongings in a piece of cloth that looked like a used diaper tied to the end of a stick. Trout was a full-blooded Turaquoi and his tribe was "fashion oriented" to say the least, but like many young fools, Trout rebelled against the old ways. He left home years ago dressed in hemp clothing. He liked the Tom Sawyer look, always had, and would not give it up even for bootlegged Armani jeans.

Trout was small and stirred little dust on the unpaved road.

It was easy to daydream in the soft sunset that was Pooheepka's. Friendly bugs flirted with needle sharp kisses. Trout knew he would miss the town and its country folk-ups. He thought back to his days on the Low IQ worm ranch. He'd always had a soft spot for worms. They used to come and rub up against his leg when he was young.

The job at Low IQ Ranch had been his dream-come-true.

I still gotta ways to walk so I think I'll tell the story one last time, Trout said to himself. I'll tell it like it was told to me by ol' Danny Quatrell before he moved in with the herd. I'll tell it to you like he told it to me, but mind you, it's been most of a year, but, well, it all started a long time ago...at the end of the road"

The End of the Road

"Hey, Dad, where's Key West?"

"It's at the end of the road, Danny."

"What happens at the end of the road?" the twelve-year old asked.

Mud Lips paused to spit a ball of brown goo out his partly open window. "Well, Danny, from what I hear it's one crazy-assed roundabout. That's what it is. It's a counter-clockwise, liquor-laden, mud-wrestling contest. Sucks you in then spits you out. It's floating out in the water, I think."

"Sounds like fun, Dad. Are we there yet?"

Unknown to Mud Lips, the car's left turn signal was broken and kept flashing. They were in the right hand lane. Irritated drivers honked like pissed off geese when they passed the overloaded Ford Falcon that hurtled south in a cloud of catalytic by-pass and countless carbon footprints. Danny thought the drivers were being friendly and waved.

Mud Lips decided on day one that it would be easier if he told the family they were going to Key West. Personally, he didn't want to go where weird things happened all the time. But, he hoped the well-known destination would stimulate Earline and Danny to abandon life in Hinckley and set forth on a family adventure.

"Honk! ... Honk!"

"Folks sure are friendly, ain't they Dad?"

"Yup, sure seems like it, Danny."

Two days earlier, the Quatrell family had packed up their belongings, shook the mothballs off their dreams and motored out of Hinckley, Ohio, bound for Key West.

They departed on October 25, the same day a nasty F2 tornado laid a big wet hickey on the rural town of Pooheepka, Florida.

Two days later, on the 27th, a blue Ford Falcon containing Billy "Mud Lips" Quatrell his wife, Earline and their twelve-year-old son Danny, coasted to a stop at the end of a dirt road, out west of Pooheepka.

Earline put down her copy of National Perspirer magazine and pointed an ink-stained finger at a wooden address board, toe-nailed to an uprooted gatepost. The board read, "Low IQ Ranch – Home of the Wigglin' Herd."

Danny looked up from the Key West brochures he'd received in the mail, "Is this Key West, Dad?"

"Nope, it's still down the road Danny."

"But you said Key West was at the end of the road and we're here, at the end of a road, right here, Dad!"

"**A** road, not **thee** road. That's a different road, Danny."

"When are we getting to that road, Dad? "

"Someday, Danny, someday."

Two months earlier and without Earline's knowledge or consent, Mud Lips lost his job and, the same day, bought a worm ranch, sight unseen, through a men's magazine advertisement. "Millions can be made! Own a Worm Ranch TODAY!" Millions of worms, the small print read.

According to Mud Lips, he got laid off because his pressure washing business was downsizing. He was, however, the only employee. It hurt to let himself go. Earline had bugged Mud Lips for years to, "Just let yourself go!" But, when he finally did, "That was not what I meant, you dumb-assed Nimrod!" was all she could say. It was enough.

However, on this day, instead of heading for Key West, the Quatrells arrived at their new worm ranch. "Wiggling Herd? Low IQ? What the fuh ...Wiggle this!" Earline twanged and gestured obscenely from the back seat where Danny couldn't see. Earline was a big girl with a big gesture.

"Hey baby, the property was a deal, before the tornado." Mud lips twanged back. SOULED was crudely printed on a cardboard sign nearby. Something struck a chord in Mud Lips.

Danny still wanted to go to Key West, like his Dad promised, but things had changed. Key West would have to wait.

The old Falcon sputtered when Mud Lips put her in gear and gained another yard up the worm-slicked driveway. The yard smelled earthy, and the Falcon's overloaded and smoking tires lent a distinctive bouquet to the atmosphere. Even from down the hill Danny could see the back part of the house was torn away.

≈≈≈

Danny's dad chewed tobacco, Red Man tobacco. Any mention of chewing Mail Pouch made him uneasy. He chawed the dampened cud and spit most of the juice out the driver's window. Unfortunately, the window only cranked halfway down. A sticky brownness prevented Mud Lips from enjoying the additional earth-tone terrain on the way up the hill.

The Falcon coughed to a stop at the top. No one was prepared for the tornado's aftermath.

"Look at all these fucking worms!" Earline gasped and tightened her seat belt.

Pickled, baked and clearly stunned, worms covered the north side of the house and surrounding property. The worms in the hot tub were a happier shade of brown than those on the sun baked, less than fruited, plain.

Danny was sad, but curious. Not curious about being sad, but wondering why a tornado would affect worms. They were in the ground! "Who invented dirt, Dad?"

"That's a good question, Danny."

"Well, who did?"

"A good question deserves a good answer, Danny."

"So what's the answer, Dad?"

"...The answer lies in the words of Mark Twain, Danny, a famous talker."

"What did he say?"

"... Twain said ... When asked a difficult and complex question, I was pleased to be able to respond quickly. I said...I don't know."

"Oh... thanks Dad."

At twelve years old, Danny had never developed a close relationship with a worm but he was ready to give it a try.

In the time it took Mud Lips to get out of the car and take a whiz, Danny calculated that there were 1.12 million squirming livestock in, on or around the land. Danny could count anything, fast. Some said it was a gift. Some said it was bullshit. But no one ever bothered to check. Danny knew they wouldn't. Danny was smart, and always right by default.

The Quatrells faced a daunting task. The worm corrals were destroyed and thousands of worms, like fat brown spaghetti, were homeless and wiggling. Part of the kitchen was blown away. The land looked like it had been worked over with a giant toilet bowl plunger.

"Hey Dad, why's these worms so long?" Danny pointed down.

"Well, Danny, I reckon that twister wind came over top of them worm fellas and sucked them plumb out of their holes. The longest ones were the toughest, Danny. See, the long ones held on till the end, just like Special Forces guys, Danny, just like I hope you do when you become a man like me. We were all good once, Danny, all good once. Let them worms be a lesson to you son and shit, we'd be rich if we sold em' by the inch! Ha, ha, ha ... Ain't that right Earline?"

"You said shit, Dad."

"Earline?"

"I ain't stepping foot on no worms. No-siree, Bob!" Earline hollered from the Falcon.

It was quiet.

Who is Bob? Mud Lips wondered.

Danny wanted to absorb the worms' emotions, but worms have feelings some kids will never fully understand.

"Earline?" Mud Lips coached.

After listening to Earline bemoan the situation for a

few hours, Mud Lips was ready to call it quits and move back to Hinckley. But Danny didn't want to go back; he hated Hinckley and those stinky, hissing buzzards. He wanted to go to Key West. Even buzzards get to go to Key West, Danny reminded himself. He'd studied the Hinckley buzzards in school and found they migrated to Key West every winter to poop on the population at will. "I won't do that if I git there!" Danny promised himself, and Key West.

"Hey Dad, look at this!"

Mud Lips climbed out of the Falcon. The springs sighed in relief.

"Danny, what the heck are you doing? Hey! Put some clothes on, you'll scare the neighbors."

"I'm gathering up some worms, Dad, and it's hot."

"It's Florida, Danny, plus you're liable get sun burned or maybe grab the wrong worm. Might not be a keeper."

"Ha, ha, good one, Dad."

"What're you going to do with them worms, son?"

"Dad," Danny inhaled to fill his brain, "these worms are called Red Gainers. I looked them up in the brochure you hid under your seat."

"Danny!"

"Dad! ...Worms is protein, Dad, and protein is food and food is money and money is the way to get the fuck outta here and on down to Key West. We'll cook em' and bag em' and call em' Organic Earth Noodles."

"You said fuck, Danny."

"I'm a worm wrangler now, Dad...Yup, I said fuck, said noodle too. You said shit. Saddle up Dad!" Danny was growing up.

"Good point son, just checking...earth noodles?

"Yup."

"Did you ask your mom?"

"No, you do it."

"Danny!"

"Dad!"

Danny's Dad trudged through the mud and tried to tell Earline about Danny's earth noodle idea but she turned the radio up and wouldn't roll her window down. Mud Lips lost a boot on the way back. He loved Danny and had no discernible perception of reality. He simply wanted Danny to learn to read and have culture. In Danny's case it would be vermiculture.

Danny rinsed off at the hand pump, turned his backside toward the sun and put his shorts on slowly. His buns had long been sunless in Hinckley.

"Still clean, Dad, look!" Danny pointed at his shorts.

"I git it, shut up."

Danny entered the remnants of the kitchen. He dug a frying pan out of the rubble and found two quarts of cooking oil and four quarts of personal lubricant under the sink. Thank goodness the labels hadn't come off, Danny thought. He had received his campfire badge in Boy Scouts and quickly built a fire with parts of the art-deco kitchen furniture. He heated the cooking oil and tossed two hundred, hot-tub marinated worms, into the boiling oil. They were the first real Red Gainer Specials and sizzled like hard rain on a tin roof. They tasted like....

The next day, the family, except Earline, decided to take some of the "Fried Earth Noodles," to neighbors who had also suffered through the tornado. The noodles were a big hit in Pooheepka. "So fat, so tasty!" said one farmer's wife with a wink at Danny.

The days grew shorter; so did the worms. Skinny, herniated worms littered the landscape. The herd grew listless. Mud Lips couldn't say listless or chew Mail Pouch.

Suddenly, when hope grew dim, a hero appeared among the herd. Danny and Mud Lips spotted the muscular worm emerging from the scarred and barren earth near the ramshackle outhouse. Danny bent and talked to the worm. The worm twisted in the hot dirt and made letter shapes that spelled his name. His name was Duke. Once Duke knew Danny could read he continued to communicate by twisting his body into the shape of letters and numbers. His interpretation of a semicolon was hilarious.

The Duke of soil rose from the recently Hoovered earth. He was a big fella and stood, ah, laid out at 9.5 inches tall, long and weighed in at .7 ounces. After a thorough vetting, an awkward group hug and a warm, worm welcome, the Quatrells, minus Earline, took Duke on as a partner.

Duke was good with the other worms but he was a big Red Gainer and was ugly, even for a worm. Still, he got all the dirt he wanted.

At first, the lesser *papagallo* worms got up in Duke's face, only to find it was his ass. Duke took it all in stride. "Worms don't stop for nothing," he liked to say in wormglish. "Gotta feed that half," he communicated with a backward nod, "to keep **it** happy."

Local legend had it that, during the vertical suction event, Duke held his breath and curled his private parts into an unyielding ball at the bottom of his dwelling. He lived alone; most worms do.

The tornado passed slowly over the vast herd's holes. It took all Duke's worm power not to exhale. Not to be sucked, ass or head first, it didn't make much difference, out of the hole, his hole, the hole where he first met "that half," his common law partner and unsympathetic lover, the half whose name was Ekud.

Others were not as fortunate or as strong as The Duke.

Duke got to work and led the dazed, appendage-challenged herd back to their respective holes. He encouraged them to get to work, "Eat and Shit!" was the Duke's rallying cry. "I don't want to see nothin' but assholes and elbows! ... ah, forget the elbows!" He encouraged the tired and worn out *clitellatas* to return to their holes. Some newly elongated worms had to dig their holes deeper so their ass wouldn't hang out in the wind.

Mud Lips was also seriously motivated by Duke and dove face-first into the soft, dark dirt. Duke was good with people too.

"Dad!" Danny snapped.

"What?" Mud Lips said through a mouthful.

"Look Dad, I'm into bioturbation now, don't mess it up."

'Well, I guess that's better than the alternative. Don't let your mom catch you and don't forget to change hands, else you'll get Carpel's Tunnel, like me. Why don't you just get a girlfriend instead?"

"Ha, ha, good one Dad."

"I just want to help, Danny."

Danny dug Mud Lip's dentures out of the soil and washed them at the hand pump.

"It's OK, Dad. Let the worms do it, OK?"

"OK, Danny, I'll try, but I'll be damned if I'm gonna let a worm out-work me."

"Whatever, Dad, just stay in soft ground, OK? Stay around the house but away from the wiring and septic tank, OK?"

"Oh, OK, Danny, OK."

Danny bought a small herd of cats from a stoned rock farmer who lived at the terminus of another dead-end road. With patience and kitty food trails, Danny trained the feline commandos to patrol the perimeter of the worm hostels and keep the early birds at bay. But Danny didn't worry too much. The Red Gainers were a tough breed and had been known to hunt as a pack and bring down large American Buffalo stink-bugs on occasion.

Soon, fresh or fried, the newly named, Earline's Organic Earth Noodles were highly sought after both by fishermen, connoisseurs and worm enthusiasts the world over. A collectible species, each Red Gainer has both male and female organs. It is said the Gainers were first discovered in Key West during the early 1700s. Many, much larger, mutant and well-dressed descendants live there to this day.

Since each worm is, not wholly by choice, both male and female, one worm is considered a team or a couple by veteran worm wranglers, marriage counselors, airlines, fishermen and cheap motels alike.

Within the first month the Wigglin' Herd turned into money when hundreds of unexpected out of town fishermen descended on Pooheepka to fish the "Tornado Zone Tournament," sponsored by the local Moose Lodge.

It was the newest rage in the game fishing business; right up there with Bone fishing in a water spout that was the newest craze in Key West.

Dozens of boats on trailers arrived in a clouds of Pooheepka dust. Mud Lips hired a good looking, skinny girl, wearing only strategically placed bobbers and a bright pink flounder pounder, to shill Red Gainers up near the highway. She did real well, he heard. Now all he had to do was find her, and get his money.

If a fishermen was lucky enough to catch a "Tornado Trout" in one of the lakes nearby, it was gutted, soaked in epoxy and Fed-Ex'd home where the sportsman's wife toe-nailed it to a wall in the den.

In a short period of time "Earline's Organic Earth Noodles, LLC" was an underground success. Danny formed the Early Bird Research Center and attempted to crossbreed New Zealand glowworms with Florida Red Gainers. The "Mood Noodles" were designed to be sold at farmer's markets, worn as living jewelry and then buried in the garden for safekeeping.

With over fifteen bait runners and three casting recovery sites, the father, the son and the wholly Duke worked the worms hard. Duke wormed like he had never wormed before.

During the day and throughout the night Duke ate, processed, and left innumerable "castings" throughout the worm community and various charitable organizations. Mud Lips also ate and processed. He was still working on his first hole when Earline, who was not into worms and had lived in the Falcon since their arrival, died.

First, Earline contracted what she called "Dirtitis."

Then a more disturbing complication occurred. Earline learned that worms "did themselves." That unsavory knowledge qualified as the last straw.

Earline fizzled out, alone, in the old Ford while father and son were outside, busy composting. "Go worm yourself!" were her last words. She said them to herself and, of course, no one can be sure she said them, but she did.

A squad of buzzard worms circled silently below. There may have been a Hinckley above.

The men buried Earline and the Falcon in a worm-free zone out back and, in keeping with Earline's last request, Mud Lips left the radio turned up full blast. It was tuned to the only music station in Pooheepka, W-ORM- AM. "We'll put a squirm in yer worm!" was the station's motto. It was worm country after all.

Danny and his dad could still hear muffled music coming through the ground twelve hours later.

"Got your mom a good battery, Danny, she was a good woman, got her a Sears Die Hard," Mud Lips said.

"Yeah, Dad, good battery."

As a tribute to his mom the earth noodles were renamed again. They would forever be known as "Earline's Ruby Reds." The Ruby Reds were advertised to be a descendant of the *Annelides Phylumpenis* (a rock band in the 60s.) and sold well.

Twenty-four years ticked by. It was a hard life.

Danny was thirty-six and still didn't even have a nickname. Meanwhile, during those twenty-four years Duke fathered 123,461 offspring, by himself. At a certain age he got tired of the worm race and, although the front part of him hated to admit it, he was tired of "That half." He said the words quietly, with a backwards nod. "I'm tired of that half always having a headache at night. " He tried sneaking out but that didn't work. Duke wanted some strange and tried to screw a garter snake. He got hurt in the process and Danny had to put his ass in a sling. Then, one dark night, in a tragic case of mistaken identity, he tried to pick himself up. He'd burrowed a hole where someone spilled a beer, got dirt drunk and didn't recognize his own ass! After the incident, "That half" wanted a divorce. Duke argued with himself continuously and, finally one afternoon, "That half" got its divorce.

On that particularly bad day, Duke positioned himself half way in and half way out the open back door. When Danny came home and slammed it closed, Duke got his divorce. In a way he hoped his back half returned as a likeable asexual friend instead of another miserable asshole.

Years later, when Duke's front half died, alone, the Old Worm Registry down at the courthouse in Pooheepka reported that Duke was one of the oldest half-assed worms ever known to exist in Pooheep County.

Danny wanted to have the worm mounted but Duke had chosen to be cremated instead. (The BBQ grill behind the house smelled bad for weeks.) The thought of going back in a hole, even his own hole, back in the dirt for eternity, troubled Duke. "That's something people do...yuck!" It would be like burying a fish in water. Just not right.

Danny studied Darwin and Darwin studied the worm which he considered to be one of the most important creatures on earth. Dogs came in second. Man was almost last, just above fish foam.

The early worm was driven to ground during the beginning of the Industrial Revolution when man chose to use mechanical and chemical means to till and fertilize the soil rather than letting the worms do their natural work. Work, it should be noted, for which they were not respected or well compensated. "Eat Dirt," was the order of the day for a worm before the advent of machinery.

But now, with Duke gone, the farm slowly returned to its natural state. Sure, Mud Lips kept up his part, eating and processing, but it wasn't enough. Then he came down with Ben Gay fever from rubbing too much of the ointment on his back after he hurt it reaching around to scratch his ass. "Wore out a disc," he told Danny. Mud Lips was getting too old and couldn't burrow effectively anymore. His castings were shallow and sad.

Danny worried about his dad and, toward the end, hired me, Trout Bender to help wrangle the ranch.

Danny met me in the worm food aisle at the local hardware store. We got to talking and, although I was new in Pooheepka, I told Danny that I worked with worms before. Danny liked me right off the bat and hired me. He gave me a place to stay on the ranch and couldn't help but ask how I got the name Trout.

"Well," I began, "my mom, Semolina Bisquick Bender told me that, when I was born my dad, Irving "Chief Butt Feather," looked at me, eyed her suspiciously and said, 'The little fucker looks like a damn trout!' I became known as Trout. It is the way of my people."

After Trout arrived things did get a little easier. He

taught Danny the *Way of the Worm*. Trout explained that a worm wrangler wakes up at dawn and sits on the porch. Later, the wrangler gets up and puts on his clothes. Sun is bad for the skin of both worms and men. With beady gunslinger eyes, the wiry wrangler stares out across the rangelands. If nothing changes by sunset, it's been a good day and he goes inside for some grub and a native smoke. Danny was thankful for this knowledge.

As young Turaquoians and blood members of the Wannabe Clan, Trout and his classmates were schooled in worm charming, along with worm grunting and worm fiddling, all socially acceptable methods of attracting earthworms from the ground. Peeing in holes was considered poor from and not allowed! The activity was usually performed to collect bait for fishing but could also take the form of a competitive sport, interpretive dance or to help one burp. Being an Indian, Trout was trained in all disciplines of worm enchantment and harvest. It wasn't that long ago he won first place at the Worm Gruntin' Free Style Festival and Bake Sale held every year in Sopchoppy, Florida, near where he grew up.

Trout practiced for the competition in his back yard. The family worms finally got tired of his stomping and cooing and quit going back in their holes. The Worm Gruntin' competition followed ground rules set forth by The British and European Federation of Wormcharmers. Rules include a plot, no greater than 3 meters by 3 meters, a five-minute warm up period, a three-person team of charmer, catcher and counter and the demand that all worms be returned to the ground after the contest in accordance with the Standards and Practices of the British

Association of Worm Length Supporters (BAWLS).

Trout won his plot fair and square on that day of competition, but he was a rebel then and a rebel now and during the teenage years, he developed his own American Worm Freeform Finger style. The worms, and a few girlfriends, loved Trout's moves and came a'crawling!

Now, day after day, the father, the son and the wholly Trout worked the land. Things were looking up, but Danny looked down and grew tired of looking at wormholes.

Mud Lips died a few years later. Danny wrote his father's obituary. It was printed in the weekly *Pooheepka Pile Gazette*.

"Dad went down his hole one day and never came up. Saved me digging one, that's for sure."

Danny filled his dad's earthly orifice with soil from the Falcon mound while right-hand man, Trout Bender, prepared a crude wooden tombstone with these words written in charcoal.

Here lays Mud Lips Quatrell. -- It's over.
We are worms in the galactic compost heap,
Temporary residents on an orbiting mulch pile.
Have fun dad - Danny & Trout B.

≈≈≈

After Mud Lips bit the dust, many of the older worms moved off the Low IQ. They wanted to be closer to town and the newly cast condos with a scenic sewer-view and spa. Danny became depressed.

≈≈≈

On a dark, lonely Tuesday morning Danny could carry on no longer, go no further. With Earline, Mud Lips and

Duke gone there was nothing left for him except a few worm memories. Danny came to the end of the road or, at least, the end of his road. Earline used to say, "Danny, if you think you're at the end of the road, just turn around!"

A real worm puts his ass in gear and heads the other way, Danny reflected. Somehow Danny knew he would never get to Key West, the real "End of the Road." Still, for more than twenty years, Danny kept wishing, and had the Key West Citizen Newspaper delivered to his P.O. Box in Pooheepka.

≈≈≈

Over the years Danny built a commodious outhouse with the bundled newsprint. However, this morning would be different.

At seven a.m. Danny took a copy of the Key West newspaper, affectionately called the "Mullet Wrapper," from the outhouse wall and squatted. He read halfway through the Letters to the Editor, sighed, then threw himself and the paper out the door and onto the compost heap. He sighed and died. It was his last sigh before he moved in with the herd.

Trout Bender found Danny when he came to work that day. He called for an ambulance but no one could hear him. He walked back into town to wake the doctor. He disturbed half a dozen people, but there was no doctor among them and by the time he rounded up the sheriff, it was too late. Trout picked up the copy of the Mullet Wrapper Danny had been reading and tucked it in to his back pocket as a memento. Trout would miss the Low IQ.

≈≈≈

After Danny went tits-up, bit the dust, bought the

farm, shit the bed, etc. Trout packed his belongings and walked into town to look for a new job. On the inside of a grain store window he saw a faded poster. It was difficult to read. Eventually he made out the words, "hel ... turt ... circ ... 999.662-4511. A turtle circus? Trout was curious and pumped a quarter into a pay phone. He was mildly surprised by the nature of the work required but took the job and rented a room near the government center trailer complex. Now, after a year devoted to circumcising snapping turtles for the animal welfare league, his time in Pooheepka came to an inglorious end. He was fired for fraternization.

Trout was a man alone.

Two hours before leaving Pooheepka forever, he packed his things and walked towards the bus station on the other side of town.

"Everything is so beautiful." Trout spouted. As he walked, he pulled a Key West Sunday newspaper out of his back pocket. It was the one he'd taken from Danny's mulch pile as a momento. He'd read it, front to back, the previous night and suddenly, "Hoo Hee! I'll bet its even beautifuller down in ol' Key West! One-hundred years ago, Trout's grandfather Moon Bender, a full-blooded Turaquoi Indian had joined forces with a guy named Wiley Bagwidth to move an abandoned bordello from Great Guano Key in the Bahamas to Key West. That was the only fact Trout knew about his early family history.

"Yessirree, Bob! I'm a-going to Key West! Maybe I'll meet an ancestor!"

≈≈≈

Less than a mile from the bus station and Trout

finally knew where he was headed and how to get there. An ongoing series of wedgies had plagued him since he'd been in Pooheepka. Maybe they would cease down south. He was hopeful.

Trout burnt some wacky-tabacky on the way to town. Fuzzy memories of a man named Moon Bender mixed with swept back flamingoes, mud flaps and birds that bobbed for worms. His mind filled with the warm winds of forgotten desire.

Trout was not dead and could prove it. He was a keeper and confirmed the convictions of a dying breed whose abandoned forts of self-preservation made way for fearless ingenuity and seedy field trips. Bender did not know he was thinking this high level stuff, but he was. It was Trout's way. It was the Bender way.

He walked on in his own nimbus cloud. "What was that daydream all about? ... I'm calling-a Ferbil on that one!" Trout mumbled resolutely and soon more, but gentler, mumblings ensued.

Ferbil is a word, immaculately birthed by Mister Trout Bender. A compact utterance designed to explain, "The lack of an explanation," in any given circumstance. "The Benders have their way with words," Trout often remarked without being asked. Suddenly, Trout's thoughts skidded to a stop, like a skateboard in the sand. Trying to rid himself of the unexplained dream was tiring, like coughing up a fur ball. Finally Trout ceased his daily thinking exercise on a familiar and decisive note. "Ferbil," Bender burbled with undisguised gusto and popped a pop-top. "There's no other word for it, hotdammit! And, there's no excuse for this continual confusion on my end of the stick." Trout guzzled his last warm Key Deer beer, crushed the can underfoot, picked it up and headed for the rural bus station. There was no one to talk with on the way to the station.

Less than a hundred yards from the depot Trout found a dumpster and tossed the can in. A small thief, hidden in the shadows sprang out and bumped into Trout. The kid quickly picked Trout's wallet, stuffed it into his front pocket then turned and ran. The kid's quick, Trout noted and grabbed hold of the dumpster.

After twenty feet the monofilament attached to Trout's wallet, and secured to Trout's belt, ran out. The kid jerked backwards, his pants ripped apart and slid to his ankles. He went down flat, like a hog-tied calf. Trout absorbed the shock, let go of the dumpster and heaved on the fishing line. He reeled the punk in, walked over and kicked the kid in the ass, hard enough to make him spit his tongue out. Trout put his left foot on the exposed tongue, took his wallet back then released the kid. Catch and release was Trout's motto. "That kind of thing will get on your nerves if you let it," Trout said to himself, and to the punk who was still lying in the dirt trying to figure out what happened.

The bus depot smelled heavy. Burnt fossil fumes and the earthy, old book odor of poor and sometimes disturbed people traveling from one failure to the next, filled the air. How do they do it? Can they *all* be writers?

Trout passed waiting buses, standing like steel horses in a row of stalls. Primordial scents melded at the boarding docks where carnivorous passenger machines idled on hot rubber tires and waited to ingest their human cargo. The two-stroke diesel souls combusted with no hope of love except from those who abandon them, like the daily turd, at scheduled stops. Loved, only for being on time, was sparse consolation for an eight-cylinder. A bus backfired. A nervous security guard fired back. These machines must be lonely; Trout ducked and speculated. He stared at worn black rubber tires. Without prejudice, the sixteen ply tires crushed torn lottery tickets, lip stick tubes, dreams, cigarette butts and gum wrappers near the curb. Trout entered the station. No heads turned, nor did beady eyes scout his progress across the worn linoleum floor.

Trout bought a ticket to Key West at the counter. He turned, pulled his T-shirt collar up and hunched into a non-existent wind. It was his James Dean slash Tom Sawyer look.

Most people can't even spell linoleum, Trout mused and garfooned deeply. He felt good about his own self. He was making a move, a step in the right direction, a move toward happiness, he hoped.

≈≈≈

When Trout arrived at Gate Four, he discovered a small, but energetic, transport company, The Gayhound Buzz Line. The Buzz Line was operated by the same guy who owned the "Harpooned Raspberry" restaurant in Key West. Trout's ride was an old school bus painted pink. The Buzz Line motto, hand printed on the side read, "We can go Fast, but we can't go Straight." A peeling bumper sticker read, "We stop for road kill."

Homeless night bugs and other disciples of darkness circled aloft eager to dive, to suck, their measure of blood

175

from waiting passengers. A few lucky bugs drilled a drunk and were instantly inebriated. With intoxicated determination they reeled around the overhead light fixtures. Most of the bulbs were burnt out and dark fanged spiders reigned supreme in the high webbed rafters. Abandoned on the scarred linoleum, charred cigarette butts outnumbered roaches and blind bus-bums smoked both with equal pleasure.

Karmic palpitations and insistent taxi horns echoed off the damp concrete walls. Weird thoughts exploded, like microwave popcorn. Trout dug it.

"Pull up Eddie! Pull up kid!' Trout said out loud. The solid walls accommodated his desire for echo. The line was from an old black and white war movie. Eddie was a pilot, his plane had been hit and he was trying to land. Ground control called, "Pull up Eddie! Pull up kid!" but Eddie made a smoking hole anyway. Trout loved reliving the movie scene in the shower, the echo was great!

Trout Bender approached the bus where the driver summarily punched his ticket. It was a simple act and Trout was a compact man, a native. He watched his chad flutter downward to hang forever, *if there is a forever*, with other abandoned chads. It was Florida after all and forever is not that long down there.

Trout mounted the Gayhound. He picked his seat and then, with the persistent wedgie corrected, looked for somewhere to sit. With a quick glance up the aisle, he casually tossed his bundle into the overhead rack. Unfortunately, there was no overhead rack and the lumpy diaper landed on a shabby blond-haired woman, already seated, low and inside. Some of Trout's toiletries fell out including a spring-loaded nose hair clipper that he had designed years ago. It was bulky and looked a little like a dildo.

"Fuck!" the female said when the nose hair clipper landed in her lap. Trout liked her style.

Dressed in a coffee bean bag, the woman smelled like cotton candy and wore one, red, sling back shoe. The heel looked like it had been chewed off. A set of rough looking, what Trout hoped were Gaucho *Boleadoras*, balls slipped from a sack below her seat. Years ago, the Turaquoi tribal elders taught Trout to come in swinging when dealing with questionable strangers wearing coffee bean bags. He fired off questions like Ali's left jabs.

"Ah, howdy miss, I got a little ahead of myowndangedself there. Is that blood or lipstick on your knees? Rug burn? Woo Wee! Is them Bolos or bull's balls? I gotta know, you know I do, you want the window? Names Trout, Trout Bender. You hearda me? I'm a native Indian! A Turaquoi from the Wannabe clan, does that answer your question? Ring a bell? You like Bingo? What's your name, sweet baby-cakes?"

"Fuck Ya," the blond beanbag quirked in grim, but determined, response.

"Fa-kuh-yah," Trout sounded it out, "...you an A-rab?"

"Oh, god!" Beth said into her air-starved cleavage, "not A-freaking- Gain!"

≈≈≈

It was quiet, naturally, and Beth wondered if her entire life experience was the result of her Midwestern accent when she said, "Fuck Ya!" She said it like the old farmers said it. She meant it like the old farmers meant it and said it hundreds of times with great sincerity.

It always worked for the farmers but never seemed to work like it was supposed to for Beth.

She *was* of Scottish descent and, wait a minute, she thought, maybe it's because there are no R's to roll in "fuck ya." Maybe that's why it doesn't work so good for me. It was all she could figure, but it helped. If I said "fuck off," would they think I was Russian?

Fortunately, real-time paused and allowed Beth, to once again be known as Fakyah, a moment to catch her breasts. Hold on, no one is gonna call me that except Blu. I gotta fix it, she said to herself.

"How the hell did I get here?" The shabby blond croaked up at Trout.

"Do you know where you're at?"

"Earth," Fakyah said with trademark conviction.

This question, "How the hell did I get here?" is often asked but rarely answered by any empirical data. It was, however, a familiar line of inquiry and occasionally uttered by Trout Bender himself, for whom the pursuit of an unanswerable question was a source of welcome relief and personal amusement, like watching women mud wrestlers.

Trout had his way with words and the newly minted Ferbil was his current and willing lover. He worked with the word on the way to Key West. It was a new day and a new way. A day when a Ferbil, in Fakyah's clothing might come into play.

The bus driver, wearing a grass skirt and combat boots, popped the clutch and Gayhound lurched forward. Trout did not have a grip, on anything, and landed a full-tilt groiner on a metal seat frame. Time stood still. So did

Trout. Finally, Bender impregnated his mind with the "Ferbil Concept," and a full and clear lack of understanding was almost his until the pain at the point of impact clouded his perception. Still, within seconds of deep impact, Trout coughed heartily, hitched his pants, cowboyed-up and twanged, "Howdy miss, names' Trou..."

"I know your name; you just introduced yourself, Nimrod." Beth said. The bus filled with exhaust fumes. "Stanks, don't it? Look here, mister... Trout Blender,"

"Ah, it's Bender." Trout rubbed the pulsing point of impact.

"OK ... HEY! Stop that, you freeking Pree-vert! ... I need food and air! You com-forking-pren- do?"

Trout didn't speak Spanish, he'd have to learn when he arrived in Key West, but somehow knew to reply, "Si!"

"You know a gas station with a mail box, bag food and a good air pump? Got any quarters? You like chicken parts, Spout?" Fakyah queried.

"I..."

"Well, let's get going then, Stout Gender!"

"Ah, it's BENder."

"OK, Grout Mender. I need air!"

"Fakyah, it's freaking BEN-der!"

"Whatever, I thought you said your name was Trout. Anyway, mister Freaking Bender, we'll get off at the first stop and eat. I got thangs to do, down on highway number one and, if you promise to grab me some ketchup packets when we git there, I'll tell you a story on the way down the Keys. You know, I've had a pretty rough time of it lately what with the gorilla, bullets and the bull and the snake, and three balls ... and .... Well, OK, mister Gout Tender!

179

You gonna help me or snot?" Beth was having fun with words for the first time in a long time.

"Ah OK, I'll help but, to be honest, you look and smell a little rough there, Fakyah. I mean like, real rough, and real smell, you know what I mean? "

"Yea, I do baby... So ... Drink me pretty, Stout Gender!" She laid open her face and pulled a bottle of Southern Comfort out of a brown paper bag that was wet on the bottom.

"Holy bat shit!" Trout smiled and sat down next to her. He looked sideways at the girl's puckered, stop-sign lips and pushed on the floor with his right foot. "I need air!" Beth bleated. Her little pink tongue tip remained out, snug between her lips. Trout pushed her tongue in, leaned over and blew down the front of her dress. "Here's some air, darlin'..." The gesture reminded her of Blu.

Beth sighed, got supple and stretched. She crossed her legs and set the drag. Trout was on the hook by the time the Gayhound hit the Overseas Highway. Beth liked Trout but was saving the real thing for Blu.

After an hour of bumps, the bus screeched to a halt for a thirty-minute rest stop in Key Larvae. The parking area was slanted to provide drainage for tropical rains. So slanted, in fact, that when the bus stopped, the passengers on the up side slid off their seats and landed on the passengers on the low side. The colorful Gayhound creaked, tipped over slowly and landed on an overfull dog park dumpster. "Crap!" someone cried.

It was a mess, but eventually Trout and Beth climbed through the escape hatch. During the mêlée, Beth lost her sling backs to an overly aggressive insurance salesman.

She found a pair of flips flops on the ground near the hatch cover and put them on. Trout clutched his diaper and accidently tripped the nose hair clipper which immediately bored a furious hole in the back of Beth's beanbag. Beth didn't notice, she was busy helping push the bus back onto its wheels.

≈≈≈

When the Gayhound flopped upright, Beth wiped her hands on her dress. So did a few other passengers. Beth didn't like that. She spoke sharply to them and heaved a few dog turds, with remarkable accuracy, at the offenders. Then she looked for and found a mailbox where she deposited a bulky, hastily-wrapped package. And, there was another pimple on her mind that she just had to pop. Simple, she was tired of the whole *Fakyah* routine. That name was just for her and Blu to share.

She flip flopped around and found Trout loitering upstream. On their way to the restrooms, Beth said, "Hey, Spout Bender, let's get something straight right now, OK, Babyfish?"

"Babyfish? ... Ah, sure, OK, sure."

"OK, here goes. My name is not really Fakyah, its Beth, Miss Beth Mobley from Misty Fork, Missouri. Really. So stop calling me Fakyah and call me Beth, OK?

"OK, Bess."

"No, not Bess, it's Bethhhh."

"OK, Miss Breast Wobbly from Missing Pork, Mississippi."

"Oh, Trout, you fucking idiot!" she tweaked a smile and liked his style. Style, she thought, like an important sounding name, expensive shoes or good hair is the only thing some people have and, for some, it's enough.

"It's Sprout!" Bender bellowed.

Trout was having fun for the first time, in a long time, too. They laughed and walked toward the restrooms, engaged in silent conversation.

Two flushes later the pair headed for an all-night Burger Thing across US 1. Beth distracted the clerk while Trout stuffed ketchup packets down the front of his pants.

He had offered to buy her some food but she seemed appalled at the idea of paying for something that quote, "Ends up being a turd." Unquote.

The caper went well until Trout remembered he wasn't wearing underwear. Suddenly, the burly manager appeared in an apron and hair net. He wasn't wearing underwear either. He caught Trout red-handed, standing among a pile of red packets with a red face. Trout looked for Beth. She was gone.

Trout had been in tough situations before, and got his ass whipped every time. But this time, he thought, this time I'll fight back! This time will be different!

It wasn't different. Trout headed back toward the Gayhound to lick his wounds, which would be virtually impossible without being a contortionist. He had some meds to ease the pain but he, Trout Bender, was tough and despite persistent rumors, *could* find his ass with both hands. He did so, gently, and sat down.

"Got the packets?" Beth asked from her window seat.

"Only one."

"Where's it at?"

"Ah..." Trout shifted uncomfortably, "...never mind."

"Huh?"

"You know, its someplace, ah... inconvenient."

"Oh, shit! How are we going to eat these crackers I stole, Grout?"

"Hey, don't look at me and, hey where's them *Boleadoras* you had under your seat, anyway? Someone musta stole 'em! I'll go and tell the bu–"

"Hold up there, Trout! I mailed them thangs out on the way over here. Told you I had something to do."

"Mailed what out? "

"Mailed them thangs out. "

"What thangs?"

"Them ... *gorilla balls!* ... if you must know. Mailed 'em back to Mama Dingling's cir–"

"Gorilla balls? Mama Dingling? What the fuh? ..."

It was quiet. Several passengers shifted uneasily in their seats.

"Never mind," Beth said.

"No, you never mind." Trout garfooned deeply, "I ... I don't understand women, Beth, I swear, I just don't!"

"That's 'cause you try, Babyfish. That's 'cause you freakin' try!"

≈≈≈

The Gayhound pulled into traffic.

Beth stared at nose prints on the grimy window, the oily smears all pointed backwards, toward a life left behind. She listened to her stomach beg for greasy food and wondered if she was destined to become a Biafran.

Somewhat stunned and only an elbow's width away Trout smelled life at the legal speed and tried to understand his many conflicting emotions.

The scent of sultry fish foamed Trout's nostrils and

countless sunbaked Tiki bars flashed past the unwashed windows. He was "Babyfish" now.

A Pod of Souls

After losing Beth in Pinhole, Blu stole a 3.5-cylinder Chinese motorcycle with a detachable sidecar. He packed bread, bologna, blankets and cheese into the sidecar and made the two thousand mile trip to Key West at thirty-five miles per hour. Blu was only a hundred miles from Key West when the sidecar broke loose. It careened wildly across US 1, plunged into the mangroves and sank. A lucky gator found the floating bag of bologna. Blu fought the gator to get it back.

The wet baloney didn't bother Blu. His teeth were so filled with bugs he couldn't tell what he was eating anyway. He reminded himself not to smile so much while driving.

Blu was down to one Chinese cylinder when he hit Marathon and, in the end, pushed the ailing motorbike by hand, from Stark Island to Key West.

Blu was tired and lonely. Bagwidth wouldn't do. He parked the remains of his motorbike in the bushes down Dung Beetle Lane and headed to the Naked Bunch.

Slowly, Blu climbed the stairs. The cross-country trip had been rough on him and his orbs. He couldn't stop humming the old cowboy tune made famous by Hemorrhoid Rogers, "Happy Tails to You ...."

Blu was happy to see Perki Mellon, still behind the bar. Her left breast was wrapped in yellow police tape.

Perki smiled when Blu walked up, "It," she nodded down and to the left, "was involved in a crime." It was all she would say when Blu raised a curious, bug-filled, eyebrow.

After Perki got off work, Blu took her to meet Uncle Bagwidth.

On Bagwidth's porch they learned that Ferling had admired Perki's mom, Sophie "Big Melons" Mellon, when they attended high school together. Because of Sophie's endowments, he informed them, she was allowed to fill two positions on the high school cheerleading squad. All the guys loved Sophie and "the twins." Ferling instantly liked Perki and told Blu they could move in with him. *Mi casa, su casa! Mi shower, su shower!*

Perki slyly gazed at her nipples to see if they were on the rise. She didn't trust her own judgment when it came to men but her nipples, like little loving beagles, never lied. The beagles remained seated and Perki said she'd think about it.

≈≈≈

It was late October the Saturday before Halloween. The Saturday when Fantasy Fest, that great tropical bead debauchery, was set to begin.

That same Fantasy Fest Saturday, Trout and Beth rode into Key West aboard the Gayhound. Beth took Trout to meet Ferling Bagwidth. She knew Bagwidth would probably be surprised to see her, but he'd always liked her if she remembered correctly. Beth knocked on the front door frame and waited. Unfortunately, Bagwidth was in the shower washing thoroughly with an old loofa sponge. Beth banged again. "Uncle Bagwidth, are you in there? It's me Bet ... ah ... Fak-yah!"

" Fakyah?"

Trout noticed there were no doors. He could see out the back of the house. No back wall either. These rich folk! Trout was about to criticize the poorly trained architect when Bagwidth steamed out of the shower wearing only a puzzled look. He recognized Beth immediately and ran to give her a hug. *"Mi casa, su casa! Mi shower, su shower!"* Skilled in the ways of men, Beth had anticipated this scenario and moved quickly aside. The bare naked Bagwidth fully embraced an astounded Trout. Bagwidth's wet feet slipped, he lost his grip, clawed at Trout's shirt and snagged his dentures on Trout's belt buckle on the way down. His teeth helped stop the fall.

Trout stared at the top of Bagwidth's head, pressed into his crotch. Then, the dental adhesive let go and Bagwidth hit the floor. With no teeth to prevent a suction lock, his lips stuck to the wet floorboards. He made unpleasant noises. Beth laughed and turned to Trout, "Welcome to Key West, Babyfish."

Trout stared at the pinkish denture hanging from his buckle. The awkward moment disturbed his sensibilities.

≈≈≈

A few minutes later, Blu and Perki came through the doorway, six packs in hand. All five pilgrims stared at each other in disbelief. Ferling could only look up with one eye. Blu stared at Beth's lips. Trout stared at Perki's tits, the beagles barked, and Perki stared at Trout staring at her. Bagwidth was still stuck to the floor and stared at the Dade county pine boards.

Beth broke the stunned silence, "Blu, is that you?"

"Beth? Oh, ah... Beth! This here is Perki." Blu said with

a nod towards Mellon.

"Perki? Ah...Babyfish, this is my lover, Blu." Beth said with a nod towards Blu.

"Beth! I'm not Babyfish"

"Huh?"

"Lover?"

"What?"

"It's Trout."

"Oh."

"Lover?"

"What?"

It was quiet.

How much must we forget before it's safe to remember?

Within minutes, Beth chose Blu, Perki chose Trout and Bagwidth remained lip-locked to the floor. Careful not to trip over Bagwidth, the two couples walked out the door hole, waved and went their separate ways.

Blu took Beth's hand. He was confused as they strolled down Dung Beetle lane. "Why'd you choose me, Beth?"

"It's 'cause you saved me Blu, don't you know that?"

"Saved you from what?"

"From everything, that's what!"

"Like what?"

"Read the book, Blu. You're my hero!"

"Hero? Me?"

"You betcha, Red Rider! Come here, baby."

"Huh?"

"Come here, Blu."

He walked into her arms and fulfilled his dream, without knowing he had.

****

OVER

A 1952, twin-engine Lockheed Lodestar, originally designed to shuttle orphaned moose for the Canadian Park Service, crossed the Colombian mountain range at 14,000 feet and descended rapidly. *Mama's Rose* was painted in hooker red on the nose cone, just above a rack of commemorative moose antlers. *Mama* all but flapped her wings to stay aloft in the thick jungle air.

If the navigator could not find the landing field in fifteen minutes, *Mama's Rose* would run out of fuel and make smoking hole somewhere near *Rioacha*, on the north coast of Colombia, South America.

≈≈≈

Four months earlier, in 1978, I, Roof Durkin, the navigator, traveled to Cali, Colombia using a passport that identified me as Perry Thrust, occupation, palm weaver. The Colombian customs officer, at the Alfonso Bonita Aragon terminal, paused when I handed him my fraudulent documents. His dark eyes traveled side to side in sinister fashion. I held most of my cool. Suddenly the official reached up and...slapped the side of his face. He'd been waiting for a dengue-laden mosquito to land. I exhaled at both ends. I was in the Third World now, but who's counting.

After a night of *Mucho mas Mucho* in the shadowy

parts of Cali and twenty-four hours without sleep, I approached an old Cessna 172 high wing airplane at the Cali airport and noticed colorful native flowers painted around bullet holes in the fuselage. The pilot was already in his seat, asleep. *Capitano Mello* was etched into his faded, plastic gold badge. I reached through the pilot's window, shook *Mello* awake, introduced myself and climbed into the rear seat hoping to catch a few Z's of my own. It had been a good night on the town. I looked for a seat belt while *Mello* waved his middle finger at the control tower. We taxied, took off and flew eastward to recon a proposed landing strip for an upcoming mission.

Shortly after takeoff, I gave up looking for the seat belt and noticed there was no glass in the passenger windows. "*Mello*, where are *los* freaking windows?" I yelled into the bug filled breeze. *Mello* turned in his seat, "*No esta aqui?*" They are not here? He pulled his headset off and threw both hands up in the air to demonstrate that he was as surprised and concerned as I.

We went into a steep nosedive. "Goddammit Mello!" I burped. Mello grinned sheepishly and managed to point ahead, toward the cockpit ceiling in this case, while he regained control of the plunging aircraft. *"Dee lake, she eez one- hundred- sixty kilo-meters deez way. "* he said. *"Eet will be looking like El Corazon, Senor Roof."*

My dad nicknamed me Roof because I had a bad case of shingles when I was young and he was hung-over. But, I've covered so many people's asses sometimes I feel like a roof.

"Corazon? A heart!" I translated.

"*Si, Senor Roof, El Corazon.*" Capitano Mello thumped

his chest in the passionate Latin manner. The gesture made him cough violently and we dropped into another uncalled for negative 2-G nosedive.

"Goddammit Mello!"

Mello calmly grabbed an almost weightless film canister, snorted a powdery mixture and quickly regained control of the plunging aircraft, for the second time in less than five-minutes. I pushed my stomach back down my throat and took a tactical nap.

One hour out of Cali, *Mello* poked me awake. We circled the landing strip and, indeed, a heart shaped lake helped identify the spot. I took a back bearing towards Cali, checked our speed and started my stopwatch when *Mello* pulled another unannounced negative 2-G nosedive to impress me. I leaned out my window hole and puked up last night's *Hora Contento*. "No having dee windows eez good to be making dee pukings, sí, no, eh?" *Mello* noted with professional understanding. He casually pointed at a jar labeled *Teeps*. I stuffed a twenty into the fucking *Teep* jar and the 2- G's stopped.

Two turns around the dirt strip and we headed back toward Cali for today's *Hora Contento,* Happy Hour. I was queasy and took another tac-nap.

An hour later we landed in Cali. I was finished puking, but wouldn't forget the lake, shaped like a heart. No one said anything about other lakes.

After my aerial upchuck I was dangerously close to sobriety and decided it was time to begin, again, night games in a sinister city. It was time for a journey... a journey to the other side of sunrise.

≈≈≈

Five months after my recon flight I met up with Tony, the pilot. We shuttled *Mama's Rose* from Oklahoma to Fort Lauderdale for an overhaul and upgrade. Two weeks of rum and cokes later, modifications were complete.

Tony, a hawkish rogue with an angular grin and I, Roof Durkin, an angular rogue with a hawkish grin, headed south toward *El Corazon* aboard *Mama's Rose*.

We departed Fort Lauderdale International Airport, winged for a touch-and-go in Bimini, turned south and flew across Cuba and the Caribbean toward the north coast of Colombia. By the time they scrambled jets in Cuba, if they did, we were over Grand Cayman.

"Tony, I hope you remembered to turn the wing tank valves on. Over." I said into the headset microphone.

"Wing tanks? Ah, I think so. Ah, Over."

"Fuck! Over."

"Over. Fuck."

We crossed the Colombian coastline and climbed to 14,000 feet to clear the lower mountaintops. With no high altitude oxygen system onboard the air was dryer than a popcorn fart. Our lips split and started to bleed. It was hard to breathe, even harder to smoke. The soft-white mountain clouds looked like a co-ed pillow fight from above. Cold nipples of stone poked through the feathery billows below.

"Shit!" Tony said for the hundredth time.

Tony continued to display a limited vocabulary during our trans-Caribbean flight. "Why didn't you mention the fucking mountains, Roof? ...Shit!" He said it again, spattering blood on the windscreen. "Over," he gagged.

"You're the pilot. Over."

I silently confessed to slackness and turned my headset volume down to muffle Tony's crass exclamations and painful observations.

Soon, the grim Sierra Nevada de Santa Marta Mountains fell behind. We descended to three-hundred feet over scrubby terrain and flew the NOE (nap of the earth) in case the army decided to set up its only working, steam powered, radar unit. I was excited but, according to Tony, "...too stoned to know which way is up." Unquote.

I knew which way was up. "Hey, Home-Fry, when you're going down, UP is hard to miss! Over."

"Home Fry? Good point, though, Over." Tony glanced at the fuel gauges, "Shit!"

I chuckled at his painful lack of imagination and tried to eyeball a safe place to put *Mama* down. We'd have to hike out of the jungle, if we survived the landing.

"I gotta get Mama on the flat, Roof, before she digs her own grave. Tally ho, Muthafuka!" Tony looked at me," Get ready to die, Roof. "

"How? ... Over." I snorteled.

The cockpit intercom hackled. Tony pressed the transmit button, "Not everything is funny, you know. Over."

"I know. Over" My chest constricted with laughter.

"Well, if you know, then why do you think everything is so fucking funny? Over."

"I don't know. Funny makes me laugh. That's why I don't read the Bible. Over."

"What? Why not? Over."

"It's not funny. Over."

"What? "

"You know, floods and famine and hell and harking angels. And all that guilt shit really kills the buzz. Bums me, man. That kind of shit is-not-funny. Period. Over."

"You're kidding me, right? And what's so funny about crashing into the jungle and dying? Over."

"Nothing, but since we haven't crashed and died yet, it seems funny talking about it and exactly how do you, quote, ' Get-ready-to-die?' You're funny as a fart in a deep-sea suit. Over." My belly hurt.

"Jesus, I'll be glad when this trip is over. Over."

"You're breaking up...reducing squelch level... say again last transmission. Over."

"Shut the fuck up. Over."

"Say again last ..."

Yes, the reconnaissance flight seemed a little blurry at this point in time and Tony was a funny guy but he started to get on my nerves. However, being the navigator, it was my job to find the lake and "do windows." Since I couldn't find the lake, I decided to clean the blood-spattered windscreen. A few energetic swipes with an old snot rag dipped in Mount Gay rum and ...SHIT! There in front of us was the heart- shaped lake, *El Lago de Corazon*. There is a god! I checked the compass bearing and VORTAC signal. The Cali radio beacon was directly on the reciprocal course!

"Hoo Boy! Over!" I crackled over the intercom.

"Who's Roy? Over?"

"That's it! Over." I pointed and jammed my finger into the windscreen.

"What shit? Over?"

"The Lake! Over." My finger throbbed.

Tony ripped his rotted leather headset off and looked at me, one foot away, in the co-pilots seat, "What fucking cake?"

I pulled my equally rotted headset off and stuffed my throbbing finger into my armpit. With clenched teeth and my good hand, I wiped Tony's bloody lip spatter from my new Ray-Ban, gold frame, real aviator sunglasses. "Look down Man! It's the damn lake. OO-Fucking-Verrrrr!" Instinctively I pointed at the lake and jammed my finger again. "Dammit! Over."

"You don't have to say "Over" when we are talking face to face you fucking idi–" Tony mumbled ..."Oh! The lake ...the lake! It looks like a Rorschach test to me, reminds me of a puss ... "

"A roach test?" I asked. "Over."

"Never mind ... Let's do it Roof, we're running on vapors!" We shook hands.

"OUCH! Let's do it ... TO IT, TONY! Over."

"Stop it."

"Sorry. Ov–"

We put our headsets back on.

I butted out a spliff and burnt a hole in my new cargo pants. The smoldering canvas smelled bad and I hurt myself trying to put the ember out. It was a bad sign; I'd made my own, "Smoking hole." I cracked the co-pilots window. The visibility improved quickly but the draft sucked the rolling papers and air chart out the opening.

There was, however, one problem in advance of all others. On our down-wind approach we spotted a dozen cows grazing on the dung-spattered landing strip.

"Cows. Over" Tony reported.

"Roger on the cows. Over." I crackled.

"Bull shit!" Tony used a different word! It broke the monotony; it was time for fun.

"Probably some cow shit too. Over." I replied with razor sharp wit and took advantage of his good mood by firing off a few pre-death jokes.

Tony ignored me. With a set of balls a professional bowler would admire and only three-hundred feet of hot air between us and South American dirt, Tony snap-rolled *Mama's Rose* onto her port wing. "We're going in!" We were light and low on fuel. Tony buzzed the scrawny cows close enough for us to see flies swarming around their boney butts.

"You forgot to say Over. Over." I noted.

All external noise faded as we angled, ass-first, toward the terra firma. On our next downwind pass Tony reached between his legs.

"Not now, Tony! Let go of that thing. It'll grow. Over." I quipped, knowing it would probably be my last good joke. Tony ignored me, again, grabbed a fuel valve and dumped gas out of the port wing tank. Then he grabbed a flare, lit it and tossed it out his window at the end of the run. The cattle hobbled out of the clearing and the dry grass didn't stand long under the fast flames. The smoke gave good ground wind direction and cleared quickly. Plus, as Tony pointed out, "Less fuel onboard and a non-flammable landing strip will improve our chances of surviving...Roof...Maybe... Over."

"Roger. Over."

From three-hundred feet the field looked like a giant cookie sheet, speckled with smoking dobs of half-baked brownie dough. The fire sputtered-out near the succulent jungle foliage. We turned into the wind for final approach. With another unnerving snap roll Tony leveled out, "Full Throttle! Full Flaps! We're going in! Fuck, Roof! Reminds me of Nam, Man!" He laughed through bloody lips.

"Yeah, Tony, me too but, enough with the snap rolls, Okay?" I adjusted my lopsided Ray Bans and tightened my harness.

In a bloody mist of vocal prayer we turned final approach, clenched our clenchables and augured into the fertile pasture. It didn't take long to realize we were alive and intact, but the cockpit harbored an undisclosed and unpleasant odor. I stared at the smoking cow patties surrounding us then, suspiciously, at Tony.

"What a landing! Hot shit! "Tony grinned and pointed proudly at his chest with his thumb.

"Yeah, you bet it is. And you forgot to say over. Over."

"It's OVER, you fucking idiot!" Tony yelled. "Take that damn headset off, Roof!"

I waited.

"I'm not going to do it, man! I'm not, I mean it. Goddamit Roof ... OK, Over. There, are you happy? ... ah shit ... OVER."

"Roger, out." I pulled my headset off, fingered my ears and climbed out of the cockpit. "Well, okay, here we are."

Tony's face was beet red. Must be altitude sickness.

"Really? Roof, the Fucking Genius."

"Do I detect a less than positive attitude, a neh-ga-teeve note of cynicism, man? Come on Tony, we made it, lighten up. Over. Just kidding, just kidding."

Years ago Tony worked effectively for Brother Louv

and the Zion Coptic church and was, in my opinion, still spiritually inclined. Being alive appeared to add to his immediate devotion and I took advantage of his weakness. "Positive vibration, ooowee ... pos-ee-teeve," I droned in my best Bob Marley and made a few dread reggae moves.

"Yeah, I guess you're right, Roof, we made it. Now all we got to do is get back. Cake- fucking-walk."

"Yep, you got that altogether, Tone. Let's check out the bush, man."

"Jesus, I'll be glad when this trip is over, I mean-really over," Tony mumbled.

"Huh?"

"Nothing."

I reached into my backpack, grabbed a snub .38 and put it in my pocket. I never go dancing in the bush without a partner.

We clambered across the smoking earth, playing hopscotch on smoldering cow turds. It was fun. It was getting dark. I wished I had not worn flip-flops. Natives were nearby. I could hear Jimmy Hendrix on a distant boom-box.

Curious eyeballs hunted our jerky progress. We approached a crude Tiki hut. A single dangling fly strip was full and unmoving. Hundreds of tiny legs flailed helplessly. Attorney flies circled, trying to eat each other while consoling the doomed. A cow mooed at a monkey and a small jungle dweller slipped out of the bush. He wore a paisley loincloth, his dick was stuffed into a Budweiser coolie cup and his bony left arm sported a crude tattoo, Cap Tony for Mayo...

"Are you from Key West?" I asked.

"*Como?*"

"Perry?"

The native looked at his feet.

"Shut up Roof, let me handle this." Tony pulled a blood-filled bug off his ear and ate it. It was a Nam' thing.

"*Mucho* bugs, *no, eh?*" Tony said and spit out seven spindly, still moving legs, one at a time. He smiled at the groinally-festooned native and burped.

"*Si senor, mucho* bug. *In español, dee* bug *is to be called 'El bicho,"* no, sí, eh?

"*Si, mas mucho* bugs *esta aqui.* Life's a *bicho, no?*" Tony winked at me, cracked the bug's shell with his incisor and continued with a grin, "*Si, mas muchos* bug *esta aqui, sí, no, eh?*"

The small brown native looked like a rusted garden gnome but stayed in the game. Even the diminutive dick-Bud knew better than to fuck with a bloody-lipped, white-assed, bug-eater.

After a few minutes, however, Tony started losing ground to the gnome. He picked his teeth with the last bug leg and remained locked in a mindless, but heated, debate with the four-foot Guajira Indian. The subject, "How many fucking bugs are on or in "*El Mundo?*" I stepped forward to cover Tony. He was not good with numbers.

"*Buenos dias, senor"* I charmed in.

"*Buenos dias, deek-brain.*"

That was uncalled for. "Hey, Tonto, if you're thinking about fucking with me you might as well go over there, lay down, grab your coolie and die comfortably... save yourself a gringo ass-kicking...You com-fucking-prendo?" I said, to break the ice.

"*Si, mucho* bicho." The jungle gnome turned to other natives milling about in the bush and made a mock face of fear. They covered their mouths and coughed politely. "*You are El Picaro, no, sí, eh?*" Coolie crotch asked.

I didn't know what *Picaro* meant but assumed it was a compliment. How could I not impress a toothless, four foot Indian in the bush?

"*Si*, EL-PICK-A-ROW. Ah, anyway, look, we're here to establish a new trading route between your piece-of-shit truck, parked over there in the bush," I pointed, "and our piece of shit plane parked over here in a pile of Cow Shit!" I swatted a bug big enough to make a Happy Meal and pointed at *Mama's Rose* with my injured finger.

"*Si, mucho bicho.*" The Indian glanced hungrily at my swollen digit that looked too much like a Vienna sausage for my comfort.

"All right. It's simple, its business, it's American, it's fun, it's getting late, so let's load this flying condom and wrap it up for the day."

"*Si, no problemo.* Dark eez good for making dee crime, no, sí, eh?"

"Grassy-ass, amigo." I gave the Indian my personal, autographed, Fong Dynasty, real woven bamboo Chinese finger trap as a token of our friendship. He put his finger in one end, his dick in the other and wandered into the jungle quite animated, amazed and unknowingly vulnerable. I winked at Tony. "White man's medicine." I explained.

"Fuck it. Over." Tony swatted a bug and left it uneaten. He was miffed. We kicked the gnome's abandoned coolie cup in awkward silence and shuffled back toward *Mama's*

Rose.

The Indians loaded the pungent burlap bales in less than an hour. I started to close the cargo door when a smoking truck pulled up and two-dozen chickens, compressed into four bamboo crates, were loaded on top of the cargo. "Deez pollo is for making dee good luck, sí, no, eh," the chicken stacker advised and, either made the sign of the cross or, crudely scratched himself. He was short, it was hard to tell.

The peeping cluckers took up more space than they were worth and would be hard to cook in-flight. The first thing I'd have to do is hold them out the window by their feet just to get the feathers off but, hopefully, the cargo they camouflaged would make them more palatable in the end.

It was getting dark. Tony and I knew we were in heavy air, over gross and could not make 14,000 feet. We would wait until daylight for fuel and good light to weave through the mountains and those hard body, co-ed clouds.

Back in the plane we pecked at some popcorn, drank water, scratched a spot on the floor and slept a troubled sleep. Fucking, clucking chickens.

≈≈≈

Just before daylight an unwise rooster crowed.

Tony snap-rolled out of a deep sleep, reached into the rooster's cage, grabbed the offending bird by the neck and milked a loose, but primo, Colombian bud down its gullet. Tony rolled over and went back to sleep. So did the rooster.

I woke up laughing but, within an hour, it was too hot to sleep or laugh. Not everything is funny, you know. We got up, poured some Mount Gay on a hundred bug bites and made ready for takeoff. Our fuel had arrived during the night. Tony and the Indians dumped sixty US Army surplus, five-gallon jerry jugs into the wing tanks. I poked a few cow turds off the nose gear and rolled a farewell, *Adios,* bye-bye spliff with a page from my fake passport. A few pokes, a few tokes, some warm Cokes and it was time to go.

Tony completed his normal pre-flight inspection that consisted of trying to do a chin-up on a wingtip. Back in the cockpit he hesitated then, reluctantly, put on his headset. "She looks good to me, Roof, let's turn and burn."

I waited.

"Over, godammit!" Tony bellowed.

"It's going to be tougher than petting a fish, but we CAN DO, man! Over"

"Stop yelling in the microphone. Over."

"WHAT? Over."

My 'Over' was beat down by the sound of *Mama's* ancient radial engines firing off. Fuel, smoke and toasted dung perfumed the low jungle air.

"That smells funny. Over." I said.

"Not everything is funny, you know? Over."

"I know."

The engines droned and Tony waited...

"Hoo Hoo! OK, you got the Roofster, Mister T, hyphen, Bone ... OVER." We were having fun now!

Tony shook his head and pushed the throttles forward. He taxied *Mama's Rose* onto the crisp dungway. There was no wind, not good; consequently it didn't make any difference in which direction we took off. *Mama's Rose* taxied to the end of the clearing. Tony spun her around and stood on the brakes. I punched the control levers, "Full pitch, full mix!" Tony hit the throttles. The old engines clattered like a bra strap in a dryer. Tony let off the brakes. *Mama* started to roll but even with her Lockheed heart she couldn't get off the ground. Not having a choice made our next decision simple. Tony punched a brake and waltzed *Mama* around again. He kept *Mama* moving through the turn to keep our speed up. "Well, that didn't work out too well, "R-Bone," let's try it again, going the other way. Over."

I grabbed the control levers, "Should I toss those clucking chickens? Over."

"Negative. Try to get them to flap their wings... you dumb fuck, Over."

"Balls to the wall, baby to Mama, we're coming in! Over." I transmitted.

"Stop that shit, will you?"

With six levers at the stops, *Mama's Rose* groaned like an old whore on a double shift. Tony let off the brakes, the RPM gauges redlined and we hurtled across the brown, pimpled face of the earth. With no runway remaining, Tony wrenched back on the steering column. Just as he yelled, "Flaps up, gear up!" we hit a palm tree and drove a frond through the nose cone. Luckily, the moose antlers absorbed most of the impact.

"That's not good. Over." Tony said.

"That's bad, but not as bad as that. " I pointed at the oil cooler outside Tony's window. It was full of straw and fire-baked cow turds. So was mine.

"Musta stirred it up on the first pass. Over." I said.

"No shit. Over. "

"Yes, shit. Over. "

"You're a real suppository of information, man." Tony shook his head. He must be having trouble clearing his ears I thought. The cockpit filled with a stomach-turning stench as the cow turds burnt off.

Suddenly, Tony ripped his headset off and stuffed it out his window. He hit the autopilot button, stuck his fingers in his ears and stared intently ahead. The oil coolers smoked as the debris burned away.

I daydreamed that someday an Indian, wearing Tony's headset as a status symbol, would stumble out of the bush and amaze a National Geographic expedition that had arrived with the well-funded intent of locating the last untelevised, naturally naked tit on the planet.

I could see the Santa Marta Mountains in the distance. They looked big. At one hundred forty knots and 10,000 feet we pierced the accumulating cumulus. Our radar was broken. "Could be the palm tree. Over." I said to no one.

We were flying VFR, visual flight rules. For mental support I called home base on our secure single-side band radio. "Baby to Mama, Baby to Mama, Come back Mama. Over." The mountains ate my words.

The engines overheated and the oil cooler gauges were redder than a baboon's ass. Tony's lips split open again, not from dehydration, but yelling from "Shit!" (What else?), every few minutes. I could barely hear him; I'd kept my headset on. I pointed at the discolored windscreen and dug out the old snot rag. The Mount Gay bottle was almost empty. I inhaled, took the last slug and sprayed it on the windscreen with my dry, puckered and now stinging lips. I wiped. Windows done, I cut a slice of burlap from a nearby bale and wrapped it across Tony's mouth like a Jesse James outlaw mask. Now he could yell "Shit" all he wanted and still see ahead. "Good moof, Roof," he muffled.

With no other choice, we elbowed through the high cotton clouds, only five hours to our refueling stop. A large grey shape appeared outside my starboard window. "What's that?" I looked at Tony.

He leaned over, lifted his outlaw flap and put his mouth to my earphone. "It's called Cumulus Granite," he bellowed.

Tony's bloody mouth stuck to my headset and pulled it away from my ear. Almost immediately his lips lost suction and the headset returned with sickening snap. I was dizzy for a moment and self-medicated. "And Yay, though I fly through the valley of stone, stoned, I shall fear no weevil." I garbled through a cockpit cloud.

"Stop laughing and quit smoking the damn cargo, godammit! Not everything is funny you know." Tony bellowed.

"I know. Over."

I pulled the snub .38 and punched out the oil temperature gauges with the barrel. I was tired of staring at the redheaded sisters of doom. I unbuckled, got up to take a whiz, stumbled over a chicken crate and accidently fired a round through the fuselage, near the cargo door. Our one-gallon piss jug got buried during the loading and I'd been wondering where to seek relief. The bullet hole provided a small, though convenient, facility.

I moved back to my seat with a sense of celestial achievement and reached for my headset. "I thought you'd shot yourself." Tony said with uncalled for joviality.

"Nope, but it was one hell of a whiz."

He shook his head. I couldn't hear his reply and focused on finding something to roll with.

"If we're going to die, we might as well die high. Over." I yelled across the cockpit.

No response. I tore a page out of the mimeographed flight manual, gathered a few stray buds and rolled a fatty. I showed it to Tony. "Say high to Baby Ruth!"

"Getting high is not going to help our altitude, Roof."

I pulled my headset off. " Yeah, you could be right Tony, but my spirit will soar, even if my ass doesn't." I put my headset back on. "You?"

"Huh?"

I glanced at the licked edge of the page and read the faded words, "Procedures for ditching at sea." I fired up the dog-eared spliff and hoped Tony wouldn't notice the print. I handed it to him, licked edge down. The clouds thickened, inside and out. We joked and toked while the oil coolers smoked.

With only the sea for company, we flew north, high on dhope.

Tony stared ahead, like a sniper without a gun. He exhaled slowly and smiled a Buddhish smile. "Roof?"

"Yeah, Tony."

"It's beautiful up here, isn't it man?"

"Yeah, Tony, it rightly is."

"Hey, Roof?"

"Yeah, Tony."

"I hope we make it."

"Why didn't I think of that?"

"Not everything is funny you know," he said softly.

"I know."

The starboard engine coughed like a chain-smoking hooker in a biker bar.

Tony looked over. "Roof?"

"Yeah, Tony."

"Roof, if things go bad man... save a bullet for me. OK?"

"That's not funny, you know."

"I know."

"Not everything is funny, you know." I couldn't help myself.

"I know! " Tony looked at me and smiled again. The starboard engine backfired with a crack and the chickens started cackling.

"Roger on the bullet, Tony. Over."

BULLET HOLES IN CANADA

Oakley Holmes Perkins sat in the back of a eighteen - foot Old Hickory wooden canoe. His wife of fifty years, Ethel Allyn Perkins, sat in the bow. Their Indian guide named Too (he didn't know how it was spelled) floated nearby in his canoe.

Oakley and Ethel were separate, yet together, as they had been since the first day of marriage. Oakley, an avid fisherman, hunched over and concentrated on untangling a bird's nest of monofilament line from his reel. Ethel, a determined novice who preferred needlepoint to fishing, felt an urgent tug on her rod. She began reeling; quietly hoping the fish would get away. Abruptly a large fish came to the surface with an attitude and, before Too could yell "STOP," Ethel heaved on the rod.

Ethel Allyn's frail arms flapped like uncooked chicken wings as she dragged a four- foot Gar Pike into the canoe. The powerful fish resembled a barracuda, its razor teeth flashed and thrashed. Its slimy body beat a fearful dirge in the early morning air.

Oakley set aside his Gordian mess and reached down the front of his pants. The Indian, Too, looked puzzled and embarrassed, *the White man*, he thought, shaking his head inconspicuously. A second later Oakley pulled a long barrel .22-caliber pistol out of his Abercrombie and Fitch's and fired three shots into the flailing fish.

"You're OK, Ethel, you're safe!" Oakley boomed. His manly voice echoed across the still waters. Gun smoke hung in the air. There was a gurgling sound.

Ethel wanted to feel safe but remained unconvinced as the canoe filled with cold Canadian water. Her belongings were swept away and began an unintended journey down the Magnetawan River. And worse, Ethel's colorful unfinished needlepoint on frame was clearly visible as it was sucked into the white rapids downstream. She couldn't help but wonder if her work would become part of a beaver dam. The canoe sank to the gunwales. Wood floats and Ethel remained steadfastly in her seat until rescued by Too in his canoe.

IT'S BEEN A PLEASURE

I was in the reception room reading and overheard.

"It has been a pleasure speaking with you this afternoon, Mrs. Weiner-Wood. You made distinct, if not noticeable progress during our session." Dr. Silo Cornhull tilted his zero-gravity chair upright. "I'm afraid our time, our precious time, my dear Mrs. Weiner-Wood, is up for now... for today...Ah, Mrs. Weiner-Wood, Mrs. Weiner-Wood? Shit." The doctor opened the door and yelled toward the front office, "Will SOMEONE please wake up Weiner and drag her ass out of here, godammit!"

Moments later Dr. Cornhull took a series of deep yogish breaths and patiently held the door for Mrs. Ethyl-Smythe-Weiner-Wood who, at age ninety-seven, was gently frog-marched toward the portal by two burly nurses.

A brief scuffle ensued at the threshold when Mrs. Weiner-Wood discovered she slept through her entire session. "My goodness! Well, for land's sake! It seemed such a short period of time," she recalled, for an instant.

After a few moments of reasonable counseling, Cornhull tired of old Weiner's whining and hypnotized her with his middle finger. Back and forth, back and forth with the finger as he glanced around the room for a sign. He saw me and the pile of magazines on the floor at my feet. Gently, Cornhull turned and told Mrs. Weiner-Wood that she was, "An elegant Victorian end table and should act like one in order to be happy." He forgot to tell her he had set her watch ahead by forty-five minutes while she napped. He loved the old ones.

Mrs. Wiener-Wood drifted further into the waiting room and got down on her hands and knees next to me. I pretended not to notice Weiner-Woods' sudden reconfiguration. I finished reading tattered pieces from a Pent Up House magazine that, according to the cover, was thirty years old. The centerfold was long gone, the yellowed pages brittle with age. "Wind is moody. Waves never tire. Horizons are everywhere. Sex comes down to friction." Those were the only words I had time to read before the magazine fell apart and slipped to the floor. Without warning Wiener-Wood stuck her tongue in the wall socket and went bacon flat. I heard her plaintiff cries but didn't want to pry and put the magazine down on Wiener's wrinkled, but completely serviceable ass.

I waited. Finally my name was called, "Mr. Gamble, please."

"Present." I responded. It was time for my appointment.

Amidst the stench of toasted wrinkles, I was introduced to my new psychiatrist, Dr. Silo Cornhull, BFD. "Poor Mrs. Weiner-Wood," he said without passion and fanned the air in front of him.

Cornhull put an arm around my shoulder and, before I could speak, moved us swiftly toward his Zero Gravity chair. "I do hope you'll excuse my use of that particularly convenient and time-tested technique but I do, I must admit, take a rather cavalier view of my patient's problems. I find it helps me not to become too... too deeply involved with situations that, let's face it, in, at or near the end, are probably irreparable anyway. Why chase a water buffalo into the bush if you're not going to shoot it? Am I right?" He fended off and landed in his chair, leaving me adrift in the room.

"Right, I guess." I replied.

"Would you care to sit?" He pointed at a beige beanbag chair in the corner.

"Thank you."

"Anyway, I understand you have an appointment."

"That's why I'm here."

"Very well, I'm quite clear."

"Queer?"

"No. Clear."

"Oh dear!" I pretended to dig wax out of my ear and slid into the comforting folds of the beanbag. No wonder old Weiner -Wood nodded out.

"What's the problem?" Cornhull inquired.

"I, its, well, its, I just don't give a fuck, anymore, I think."

"Ahh. I see."

"See what?"

"I see that you don't give a fuck."

"About what?"

"About anything, anymore."

I was dealing with a big brain here.

"Uh, that was a quick summation of a complicated

problem."

"It's what we call a Sabaki." Cornhull skillfully countered.

"Sabaki?"

" A Sabaki, Mr. Gamble, is a mode in which the objective is to deal effectively with the local situation, avoiding longer-term problems, a quick and efficient solution to a complex and difficult problem, perhaps. It's Japanese, you know. Plus, you only paid for 15 minutes."

"You're working without a net, Doc."

"I know. "

"Hey wait a minute! It's a fucking Sabaki, right?"

"Right! We should be happy indeed Mr. Gamble!" Doctor Cornhull applauded and reached for an ergonomic armpit flask. I, in turn, pulled out a resinous and well-rolled bone of contention.

After our enhanced session, which Cornhull considered a success, I gave the doctor ten singles that I'd been saving for my titty bar therapy session and headed for the door. Cornhull was still counting when I left, just another brain destined to dry and wither in the blaze of earth's flaming orb ...

I left Cornhull's office and walked slowly toward my work place. I had hoped my meeting with Dr. Cornhull would produce more than a good buzz but the session was ultimately successful, I guess, because I took away a fresh concept. "I think, therefore I am... probably wrong." I'll have to remember that one. But for now, it's back to business.

My name is Willie Gamble I am the assistant manager

at Earl's Sock Barn just off Route 8 in Ligonier, Noble County, Indiana. Ligonier is the Marshmallow Capital of the World and a town where anything can happen, but doesn't.

"CHECK-OUT TIME"

... Jordan whined. "There's no little bottles of shampoo, no body lotion, no shower cap, nothing! The toilet paper isn't even folded! You cheap ass!" The crooked croupiers looked at each other.

"Chill, I'm not your mother," Alan said bravely and moved to relieve himself. "Jordan, look at this!"

"Not now, Alan." But curiosity drew Jordan to the bowl. The baseball cap and sunglasses fell to the floor.

Beneath the crystalline waters, lay a clear bag. It appeared to be filled with blood red rubies.

Alan and Jordan kneeled to inspect the sparkling stones. Each could see the other's reflection in the water. A closet door opened silently behind them. A third reflection appeared from above. The intruder slammed the toilet seat down, forcing their heads into the bowl then sat on it, patiently. Four knock-off Gucci's slapped pathetically on the cold tile. Four knees banged and contorted blue lips puckered like a prudent Koi, ready for a final kiss goodbye.

"It's sad." the third reflection mumbled and kept flushing.

Alan and Jordan died staring at each other and the stones. The water slowly turned red. Not from blood, but from rock candy rubies, dissolving.

A gloved hand dialed the front desk and asked for a late check out.

"Never did trust that kid." The third reflection mumbled, found Jordan's bag, filled it with the missing toiletries, baseball cap, sunglasses and moved quickly into the waiting darkness. The night was cold; the Vegas strip nearly empty. It was a place where fortunes changed hands faster than jumper cables at a redneck funeral.

≈≈≈

The third reflection entered the *Hy-Ball* casino. A drab purse, containing the item from Jordan's bag, hung on a drab shoulder. The Random Number Generator reader had been a difficult item to come by. Five hard years and one motel room later, a fortune lay ahead.

The purse fit perfectly between two slot machines. A human head didn't. Behind the purse flap was a small computer that looked like an I-phone. Through a tiny window on the side of the slot machine the computer read the top and bottom numbers on the RNG. It divided the top number into the bottom number and multiplied by ten.

On the thirteenth slot machine the reader showed a payoff probability of ninety-seven percent. The third reflection racked up $ 12,000.00 in a short time.

≈≈≈

Bulky men appeared and jerked the drab gambler upright. The purse was confiscated; sunglasses and baseball cap came off exposing an overweight red-haired woman. Two security guards frog-marched the rotund redhead unceremoniously toward the front door.

A nearby croupier noticed the commotion. "Hey, you're Alan's step-mom, right? He didn't come to work today, is he sick?"

"Maybe...the little fucker sure looked flushed the last time I saw him."

Without warning her overloaded heart stopped but her ass didn't. She groped the beefy bouncers, took three steps and toppled face-first onto the carpet with a thickening thump. Check out time.

Radios crackled. Gawkers gawked. The drab purse disappeared.

Thank you for reading.
Please review this book. Reviews help others find me and inspires me to keep writing!

If you would like to be put on our email list to receive updates on new releases, contests, and promotions, please go to AbsolutelyAmazingEbooks.com and sign up.

About the Author

Captain Mark T. "Reef" Perkins is a marine surveyor with a colorful past. From commanding a 150-foot 300 DWT US Army diving ship off Vietnam to smuggling in the Caribbean, Reef Perkins has become a living legend. A graduate of both the US Army Engineer Officer Candidate School and the US Navy Salvage Officers School, he's a man comfortable in or out of the water. Raised in rural Michigan, Reef now lives in Key West where he can get his feet wet. He is the author of the bestselling memoir, *Sex, Salvage & Secrets*.

ABSOLUTELY AMAZING eBOOKS

AbsolutelyAmazingEbooks.com
or AA-eBooks.com

Made in the USA
Lexington, KY
23 January 2014